The  se

Copyright ....on Haynes

Book two in the Hal Junior series

Stay in touch!

Author's newsletter:
spacejock.com.au/ML.html

facebook.com/halspacejock
twitter.com/spacejock

www.haljunior.com

The Hal Junior Series:

The Secret Signal
The Missing Case
The Gyris Mission
The Comet Caper

Simon Haynes also writes the
Hal Spacejock series for teens & adults

... AND the
Harriet Walsh series for teens & adults.

www.spacejock.com.au

Simon Haynes

HAL JUNIOR

THE MISSING CASE

Bowman Press

Published by Bowman Press

All Text and Artwork ©2012
Cover art by Simon and Alex Haynes
Internal Illustrations by Simon Haynes
Chapter 11 illustration by Jo Haynes

ISBN 978-1-877034-31-2 (Ebook)
ISBN 978-1-877034-25-1 (Paperback)

National Library of Australia Cataloguing-in-Publication entry
Author: Haynes, Simon, 1967-
Title: The missing case / Simon Haynes.
ISBN: 9781877034251 (pbk.)
Series: Haynes, Simon, 1967- Hal Junior ; 2 .
Target Audience: For primary school age.
Dewey Number: A823.4

Dedicated to my little brother

There was a young lad called Hal Junior,
whose homework was always peculiar.
His essays were bad,
His sums didn't add,
And his limericks weren't any good either!

— 1 —

Crime

Picture a small clearing in a very large forest. It's late at night, and the rustling trees sound like whispers in the shadows. Now imagine a camouflaged tent pitched in the middle of the clearing, and a tall, lean man in combat fatigues sitting on a rucksack.

Got all that? Good, then we'll begin.

The man was Captain Spacejock of the Intergalactic Peace Force, and he didn't look happy. He was reading a report, and his expression grew grimmer the further he read. Once he'd finished he cursed under his breath, rolled the computer up and tucked it down the side of his boot.

In the past few days they'd lost three valuable ships in this sector. Now it was four.

The burnt-out wreckage of Captain Spacejock's ship - the Phantom X1 *- could just be seen through* *the trees. Had the fearless Captain fallen to a superior pilot? Had he been jumped by a whole squadron of enemy ships? No! Random bad luck had been his downfall: A stray meteorite had punched a hole through the engine, cutting power and sending the Phantom plunging towards the uninhabited planet.*

Captain Spacejock barely escaped with his life, scrambling free just before the ship exploded. The only thing he'd managed to save was the survival kit: a rucksack containing the tent, two bottles of water, food rations, and a firestarter.

Now the tent was up it was time to light a fire. Captain Spacejock gathered some fallen branches, activated the firestarter and held the steady flame to the wood. Once it was burning he unwrapped a ration pack and –

'Put it out! Put it out right now or I'll tell!'

Hal Junior jumped, almost dropping the firestarter. 'But we have to practice!'

'They'll show us how to light fires when we get there.' Hal's best mate Stephen 'Stinky' Binn grabbed his wrist. 'Switch that thing off! It's dangerous!'

It was late evening, and the boys were in the Space Station's canteen. They'd waited impatiently while the adults finished their meals, all the time wondering how anyone could take so long over food. Eventually the coast was clear, and Hal took handfuls of torn cardboard from his pockets and piled them up in the kitchen sink. Fires were forbidden aboard the Station, what with water and air being so precious, but Hal reckoned a small practice burn in the metal sink would be okay. After all, the entire class was going to planet Gyris for a camping trip, and they might all starve if he didn't learn how to cook!

'I can't believe you ripped up my cardboard,' muttered Stinky, eying the torn scraps. 'I was saving it for craft!'

Hal snorted. 'You won't care about some cheesy craft project when you're cold and hungry.'

'You could have asked.'

'I did.'

'This isn't borrowing, it's total destruction. And you can't set fire to it. It's not allowed and I won't let you.'

Hal needed a diversion, so he pointed to the doorway. 'Look out! Someone's coming!'

Stinky didn't wait. He yanked open a cupboard and burrowed into the piles of cleaning rags and tea towels. Meanwhile, Hal activated the firestarter and touched it to the cardboard. Yellow flames licked at the rough edges, and wisps of smoke curled past his face. The smoke was bitter, and he wrinkled his nose.

Stinky realised he'd been duped. He poked his head out the cupboard, a cleaning rag draped over one eye. 'Hal! You can't! You mustn't!'

'I'm making a campfire,' said Hal doggedly. 'We're going to toast our rations.'

'When they smell the smoke they're going to toast your b–'

'Ask me why I'm doing this. Go on!'

'Because you want to get in trouble. Again.'

'No! I'm practising for the camping trip.' Hal grabbed a ration bar from the box on the counter, and ripped off the foil packaging. 'We're going to cook our own food, just like they do in the wild.'

Stinky removed the cleaning rag and climbed out of the cupboard. 'You'd better do something with that fire. It's going out.'

Hal peered into the sink and saw the scraps of card were almost gone. He blew on them until they glowed, then stuck one end of the food ration into the yellow flame. It spat and crackled before catching fire with a puff of blue smoke.

'Er, Hal . . . ' began Stinky. 'Is it supposed to do that?'

The fire spread quickly, and Hal dropped the ration bar just before the flames reached his fingers. The bar shattered in the sink and the fragments burned ferociously, filling the kitchen with smoke. Even worse, the evil-smelling fog began to drift into the canteen, hiding all the tables and chairs.

'Hal, someone's going to see it!'

'See it?' muttered Hal. 'They'll smell it for weeks!'

They stared into the sink. Lighting the fire had been easy enough, but how did you put one out? 'Quick,' said Hal. 'Think!'

Beeeeep-BEEEEEP-beeeep-BEEEEEP!

At first Hal thought Stinky's brain had overloaded, but then he recognised the fire alarm. Sirens shrieked, hazard lights flashed, and a panicky voice blared from hidden speakers.

'Fire alert. Fire alert! Emergency personnel report to the E-section canteen. This is not a drill. I repeat, this is not a drill!'

Hal and Stinky stared at each other in horror. Now they were really in for it!

Punishment

Buzz buzz!

The alarm woke Hal instantly. He'd been dreaming about the camping trip, where they'd been cooking breakfast over a real fire. There were eggs and bacon and fried tomatoes sizzling in the frying pan, and crusty bread with butter and jam for afters. Maybe even coffee, or hot chocolate! After breakfast they were going to hike through the forest and splash about in the river while a huge lunch was prepared at base camp.

Buzz buzz!

Then Hal remembered where he was going to be during the camping trip: Confined to his cabin aboard the Space Station!

Nag, nag, nag, fire. Blah, blah, blah, explosion. Dangerous. Irresponsible. Punishment.

Hal groaned and pulled the blanket over his head.

It had only been a small campfire, and how was he to know the food rations would go off like a box of firecrackers? It was so unfair! Instead of telling him off, his parents should have given him a medal for showing them how dangerous their food was!

Stinky's eyebrows would grow back, eventually, and there hadn't been any real damage to the kitchen. It was a pity about the windows, but even titchy little bits of glass could be recycled into new panes. There had certainly been enough pieces.

Buzz BUZZ!

Hal reached out to flatten his alarm, then remembered his mum's promise the night before: she told him there would be a surprise for him in the morning. Maybe, just maybe, they were letting him go on the camping trip after all! Hal threw the blankets off and leapt out of bed. He spent as much time getting dressed as he usually did on his homework - that is to say, not much at all - and when he was ready he burst out of his cabin and flew along the corridor.

Hal lived aboard a deep space freighter which was permanently attached to the side of Space Station Oberon*. The freighter would never fly again, but the old cabins could still be used for living areas and storage space. The ship hadn't

---

* *Hal Junior: The Secret Signal*

been there long and workers were still busy with the conversion, which meant Hal encountered new signs and detours every morning.

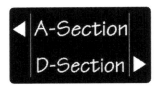
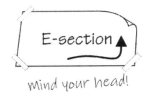

mind your head!

Hal rounded a corner, took a lift to the next deck, and arrived at the common room. His mum and dad were sitting at a table with a mug of coffee and half a ration bar each. Normally they'd eat something a bit more appetising, but the last food shipment had contained nothing but ration bars, all well past their expiry dates.

As Hal approached the table, his mum and dad pretended to shield their food.

'I'm not going to light them!' protested Hal.

'Pity,' remarked his dad. 'It might improve the flavour.'

Hal pulled a face, then turned to his mum. 'What did you mean by a special treat?'

'Morning Hal. Lost your comb again?'

Hal ran his fingers through his hair. Never mind tidying himself up! What was the big surprise?

'Remember what I said about being on your best behaviour?'

'I haven't done anything wrong. I swear!'

'And you won't either. A very important guest is arriving after lunch. His name is Hank Grogan and he's visiting the Space Station to discuss our future.' Hal's mum hesitated. 'Grogan is very rich, Hal, and his money could keep our research going for years. Do you understand how important this is?'

Hal understood all right. The other scientists were always complaining to his mum about the old equipment in the lab, and his dad barely had enough parts to keep the air filters running. It wasn't his mum's fault ... Space Station Oberon existed on handouts from all the nearby planets, and they just had to make do with what they were given. Like stale ration bars, for example. 'Mum, what is your research?'

'You know I can't tell you.'

'Is it really important?'

'Oh yes.'

Hal hoped the research was something really cool like a super fast spaceship engine or an instant teleporter, but he suspected it was something to do with food or medicine. Whatever it was, if this VIP was offering money and equipment then Hal was determined to be on his best behaviour.

His mum continued. 'When Grogan arrives we

have a very important task for you. Do you think you can handle it?'

Hal's eyes widened. An important task! Did they want him to guide Grogan's ship into the docking bay? Show him around the secret laboratory? Accept a valuable gift on behalf of the space station? 'Of course!'

'Good. We just found out Grogan is bringing his son Alex along, and we need someone to take care of the boy while his father is inspecting the Station.'

'Babysitting!' snorted Hal in disgust. 'Can't you find someone else?'

Hal's mum gave him a stern look. 'Hal Junior, this is very important. If you pull this off we'll cancel your punishment. Do you understand?'

'The camping trip?' A ray of hope shone through Hal's gloomy mood. 'You mean I can go?'

'If you behave.'

Hal weighed up the options. A week cooped up in his cabin versus a few hours looking after some stuck-up kid. What a choice!

— 3 —

The VIP

'Quick, make up your mind.'

'I'm thinking!'

'What's there to think about?'

Hal was thinking he might be able to lock the rich kid up and enjoy a bit of freedom, but the glint in his mum's eye said otherwise. 'All right. I'll do it.'

Hal's mum took his hands in hers. 'Do I need to warn you about risky behaviour? No climbing around in the recycling chutes. No games of spacers and aliens with real guns. And absolutely no fires.'

'Understood,' said Hal. 'We'll just sit and stare at the wall all day.'

'Don't be silly. I'll give you a pass for the recreation room. There are some new cartoons you haven't seen yet.'

Hal pressed his lips together. Cartoons! Did

mum think he was still five years old? Then he remembered the gaming rigs in the rec room, the ones with the virtual shoot-em-ups. Excellent! They were supposed to be adults-only, but Stinky had rigged a bypass code. A deathmatch smackdown would show this Alex kid who was boss!

```
Player One:      Player Two:
9,256,001      0,000,013
Hal Wins ... Again!
```

Fortunately Hal's mum was distracted, and she missed his calculating expression. 'Go and wait in your cabin. I'll send for you when our guests are settled in.'

'Mum! I have to be there to say hello.'

His mum's eyes narrowed. 'Why?'

'The space station can be scary for a new kid. It'll be much better if I'm there to smooth things over.'

'Hal Junior, the only time you smooth things over is when you melt them.'

'I'll be good. I promise!'

His mum hesitated. 'All right, you can come. But if you embarrass me I'll . . .'

What she'd do to him was never explained, because at that moment her commset buzzed. She checked the screen then jumped up. 'They're docking. Come on, or we'll be late.'

Flight Control was humming by the time they arrived. There was a big crowd at the docking bay windows, all jostling for the glimpse of the VIP. The only adult missing was Hal's dad, who'd turned down the opportunity to meet Hank Grogan. In fact, he left the canteen muttering that he'd rather clean all the station's air filters with his own tongue.

However, upon seeing the crowds, Hal realised how just important this visitor was to the station. He still wasn't happy about the babysitting job, but he was determined to get it right and prove he could be trusted.

The crowd gasped, and Hal pushed his way to the front to see what they were ooh-ing and ahh-ing about. When he saw the VIP's ship he oohed and ahhed right along with them.

Once a month the space station was visited by a dumpy old supply vessel. It was a converted asteroid miner, decades old, and it was as battered and patched up as a favourite pair of jeans. When someone mentioned spaceships, that was the kind of thing Hal imagined.

This ship was something else. It was sleek, nimble, and brand new. Everything about it screamed speed, from the long pointed nose to the swept-back exhaust cones. Hal saw movement through the raked canopy, and he watched the pilot going through system checks and shutting down the engines. There was a smaller figure alongside him, wearing a matching flight suit and headset, and Hal realised it was Grogan's son. He felt a stab of jealousy as he watched the pair of them working together on the controls. Was the kid really helping to fly the ship?

Still, what if the visitor let *him* sit in the sleek vessel? They could pretend to patrol the galaxy, hunting down Captain Spacejock's enemies and helping to keep humanity safe. Maybe there'd be proper rations to eat, and flight suits they could try on, and laser guns and . . .

Chack!

Hal jumped at the loud noise, and then he realised it was just the docking clamps attaching themselves to the ship's nose. Next, a flexible boarding tube extended from the space station, moving towards the ship until it covered the canopy. With the visitors hidden from view, the crowd left the windows and hurried to the airlock, where they formed two lines. As head scientist Hal's mum stood at the end, ready to greet their guests. As head babysitter, Hal pushed through the crowd to stand alongside her.

There was a hiss as the airlock door opened, revealing two figures in gleaming spacesuits. They stowed their helmet and suits in the locker, and when they were done they strolled up the boarding ramp towards Hal's mum. The VIP was pretty much as Hal expected: a grey-haired man with a tanned face, wearing an expensive-looking jacket and neatly pressed trousers. His son was about Hal's age, with swept-back blonde hair and an upturned nose, and Hal's stomach sank as he saw the snooty expression. So much for roaming the space station, building shelters and practising with the escape hatches. This stuck-up know-it-all looked like a right killjoy.

The VIP spotted Hal's mum. 'Doctor Walsh, I presume?'

They shook hands. 'Welcome to the Oberon, Mr Grogan.'

'We've been looking forward to this visit. It's great to be here.' There was a snort alongside him. 'Oh yes. And this is my daughter Alex.'

Surprise!

Hal couldn't believe it. He'd been saddled with a snooty, stuck-up girl!

'You must be Hal,' said Grogan, clapping him on the shoulder. 'I've heard a lot about you.'

'It wasn't my fault,' said Hal quickly. 'I didn't know the fire would –'

'That's enough, Hal,' said his mum. 'We don't need the details.'

Grogan laughed heartily. 'I hear you offered to show my daughter around your little space station. That's mighty good of you.'

Alex turned her nose up even higher, and Hal's stomach sank. He would do anything to go on the camping trip, but showing a spoiled kid around his favourite haunts was right on the limit. He looked to his mum for support, but she was introducing Grogan to the scientists. When she was done the adults filed out of the control room, leaving Hal alone with Alex. 'After you,' he said, indicating the exit.

Alex drew back. 'I'm not holding your hand!'

'Who said anything about –'

'I have a boyfriend. He's bigger than you and he'll punch you in the nose.'

'Well I have a girlfriend, and she could snap your boyfriend like a ration bar.'

'You do not!'

'Do so.'

'Not!'

'So!'

'Not so! You said it!'

Hal's eyes narrowed. The battle lines had been drawn! As they followed the adults up the main tunnel, Hal fired his best shot. 'I bet your mouldy boyfriend never saved a space station from kidnappers and thieves.'

'We defended three planets against an alien battle fleet. And his dad *owns* a space station.'

'I own ten of them!' declared Hal.

'In your dreams, space boy.'

Hal scowled. 'My dad's taller than your dad.'

'My dad's richer.'

'My mum's smarter than your mum.'

Alex was silent.

'You lose!' crowed Hal.

'I – I don't have a mum.'

Hal was horrified. 'I'm sorry. I didn't mean . . . '

'It's all right, it was years ago. She died in a freak web surfing accident.'

'Eh?'

'You sucker!' cackled Alex. 'You should have seen your face!'

'That's not funny! You can't joke about things like that!'

Alex shrugged. 'Mum left us when I was little. I'll say whatever I like about her.'

'You shouldn't.'

'Can so!'

'Not!'

'So!'

'Snot!'

They stopped to scowl at each other, nose to nose, then burst out laughing. Alex looked much nicer without the snooty expression, and Hal realised the day might not be a total write-off after all. 'Come on, we'd better catch up.'

'After you, space boy.'

Before long they reached the A-Section checkpoint, where a uniformed guard was standing stiffly to attention. Hal smiled at the sight. Usually the guard lounged around in jeans and T-shirt, but the Space Station was really putting on a show for their precious VIP. Then he looked closer and laughed out loud. The guard was Stinky's older brother, Richard! His uniform was buttoned up to the neck, and his gleaming gold badge looked like it had been polished all night long.

'Please display your passes,' said Richard, in a businesslike tone.

The adults obeyed, and were let through one by one. When it was the VIP's turn he showed his visitor badge and made to pass the checkpoint.

'I'm sorry, sir. I need to see inside that case.'

'It's all right, son.' Grogan tapped his badge. 'I'm a VIP. I can take this case wherever I want.'

'That's a negative,' said Richard, his eyes hard under the peaked cap. 'According to regulation nineteen slash twelve, all containers must be inspected.'

Hal's mum joined in. 'I'm afraid he's right, Mr Grogan. It won't take a moment.'

'Do you think I'm carrying a bomb in here?'

'Of course not. However, the lab is full of sensitive equipment. A stray signal from a commset, contamination from foreign matter . . . you could set our research back months.'

'But –'

'I'm sorry, but I must insist.'

'No chance.' Grogan tightened his grip on the briefcase. 'This case is full of personal data!'

'Why don't you leave it at the checkpoint?'

'I'm not letting it out of my sight.'

Hal stared from one to the other, eager to see how it turned out. Adults were usually boring, but this was real drama for a change. Would his mum wrestle Grogan for the briefcase? Would Grogan try to bust through the security checkpoint, only for Stinky's brother to shoot him with a stun gun?

But there was no wrestling or gunplay. Instead, help came from an unexpected quarter.

'Dad, why don't I look after it?'

Everyone turned to look at Alex.

'You trust me, don't you?' she said.

'Of course I do, sweetest. But I'm going to need this later.'

'So page me, and I'll bring it back here for you.'

'There you go,' said Hal's mum. 'The perfect solution.'

Grogan hesitated, then passed the briefcase to Alex. After a lingering frown at Stinky's brother Richard, he followed the others into A-Section.

Hal was impressed. The briefcase was made out of shiny blue metal, and it had a big lock on top with red and green status lights. His parents would never trust him with anything like that!

Alex noticed his admiring look. 'I don't know why dad brought this old thing along. He's got a much better one at home.'

'My mum's briefcase has wheels on.'

'My dad's briefcase can fly.'

Hal snorted. 'They all do, if you throw them hard enough.'

'That's not funny.'

'Depends who the briefcase belongs to,' said Hal shortly. He glanced up the corridor in case his mum had changed her mind and decided to take them on the guided tour. Unfortunately, all he got was a suspicious scowl from Stinky's brother. A few months earlier Hal had used Richard's entire stash of hair gel to make a slippery slide in the corridor, and afterwards he'd refilled the little plastic tubs with hull repair glue. The stuff looked just like hair gel, but unfortunately it set like concrete. First, Richard spent a week with his head encased in a gleaming shell. Then, once his hair grew out, he had to endure a really close shave. Even now his hair was still on the short side, and Hal decided it would be best not to linger.

5

Hostilities

Hal turned to Alex as they strolled away from the checkpoint. 'What do you want to see first?'

'How about the beach? No, maybe the park would be better. Or wait . . . how about the local swimming pool?'

Hal felt like suggesting a long walk out of a short airlock, but he knew his mum wouldn't approve. He tried to think of somewhere interesting and exciting - somewhere he was actually allowed to visit - and came up empty. 'Do you want to see my classroom?'

'Are you nuts? I didn't come all this way to do school lessons.' Alex thought for a moment. 'Tell you what, why don't you show me to the mall? I'll find some cool people to hang around with and you can do your homework like a good little boy.'

Hal frowned at the insult. 'What's a mall?'

'You know . . . shops, restaurants, that kind of

thing.'

Hal looked puzzled. 'Why would we need those on a space station?'

'You don't have a mall?'

'We have a supply depot and a staff canteen.'

'Sounds wonderful. So what do you do for fun?'

'We use the space simulators, and there are running machines in the gym. And sometimes we feed plants in the hydroponics lab.'

'What a boring place to live!'

'It's not boring. We do important research.'

'Oh yeah?' Alex looked him up and down. 'What sort of research?'

'It's top secret. I can't tell you.'

'Huh, I bet it's food or medicine.'

'It is not!'

'It is so. Totally boring!'

'It's way better than food or medicine.'

'You don't even know!'

'Do so!' Hal hesitated. 'We're inventing a huge teleporter. It can move planets all over the galaxy.'

Alex stared. 'Really?'

'Yes! It's so big it could even teleport your head.'

'Very witty, space bug.'

'Funnier than you, ground hugger.'

'Wormhole!'

Hal frowned. 'Dirt crawler!'

'At least I don't breathe tinned air.'

'I wouldn't use your polluted air if you paid me.'

'Who'd give you money? You can't even spend it!'

Thoroughly annoyed, Hal stormed off. If Alex wanted a tour of the Space Station she could show herself around.

'Where are you going?'

'Anywhere but here,' shouted Hal over his shoulder.

'But I don't know my way around. I could get lost.'

'Good!'

'What's your mum going to say?' called Alex.

Hal knew exactly what she'd say, and it wouldn't be pleasant. Reluctantly, he retraced his steps. 'All right, I'll show you round.' He pulled his sleeve up and inspected his big chrome watch. 'Two hours, and not a minute more.'

Alex snorted. 'Where did you get that old thing?'

Hal was scandalised. The watch was his most treasured possession, and he was convinced it had once been worn by Captain Spacejock of the Intergalactic Peace Force. 'This is a genuine space watch!'

'Yeah, twenty years ago.' Alex showed him the slim black band on her own wrist. 'This is what the good ones look like.'

'You call that a watch?' said Hal, with a laugh. 'It looks like a cheap plastic bangle.'

Alex shook her wrist, and there was a muted 'snap' as the outer skin of the bracelet unfurled into a rectangular screen. It had a menu full of icons, and when Alex tapped one a bright light shone from the middle of the device.

'Whoopee-doo,' said Hal. 'It was about time someone invented a bracelet torch.'

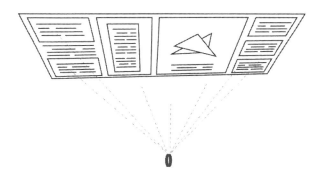

Alex said nothing. She just gestured at the ceiling.

Hal looked up and gasped. There was a huge image projected on the roof, and it was showing atmospheric pressure and air quality, the location of all nearby planets and ships plus hundreds of other variables.

'It plays movies too. I have four thousand of them. And every book ever written. And all the music.'

Hal was green with jealousy, but he'd never admit it. 'I bet the batteries don't last.'

'Batteries are so yesterday! This thing has an everlasting power unit.'

Hal pulled his sleeve down, hiding his watch. Alex was always one step ahead of him, but that was about to change. 'Come on, let's go.'

'Where to?'

'The recreation room.'

'Great. I bet it's a right old museum.'

'No, it has proper arcade machines. They're adults-only, but I cracked the access code.'

'The only thing you ever cracked was a glass window,' muttered Alex. Even so, she looked curious. 'These machines . . . what games have you got?'

Hal smiled. 'Follow me and I'll show you.'

Hal and Alex walked across the Space Station in silence, and they hadn't gone far before Hal realised Alex was having trouble with the briefcase. After all the insults he was tempted to let her struggle, but she was a guest and there was still a slim chance she might show him around her dad's spaceship. 'That looks heavy. Do you want me to take it for a bit?'

'I could carry this thing all day,' said Alex shortly.

'If you say so.' Hal smiled to himself. So she could carry it all day, could she? Very well, why not find out?

After several minutes they reached the end of the corridor, where there were two signs on the wall: one said 'D section, level 9', and pointed back the way they'd come, while the other pointed up a flight of stairs to 'D section, level 8'. Their feet clattered as they took the metal steps, and they turned left twice before encountering another corridor.

'Haven't you people heard of elevators?' complained Alex.

'Walking is good for you.' Hal couldn't hide a grin. 'Didn't you know that, sweetest?'

Alex turned a force ten scowl on him, before gripping the briefcase and forging ahead. Five minutes later they reached another set of steps, these going down, and when Alex saw yet another long corridor at the bottom she stopped dead. 'This is totally ridiculous.'

'It's not far now,' said Hal. 'Honest.'

Alex switched the briefcase to the opposite side, gritted her teeth and set off along the corridor. They walked past several doors before reaching the end, where there was . . . another set of steps.

Alex glanced at the sign on the wall, then did a

double-take. One said 'D-section, level 9' and the other pointed up the stairs to 'D section, level 8'. She frowned at the signs, looked back along the corridor, then rounded on Hal. 'Okay, what are you playing at?'

Hal's expression was pure innocence, but he was struggling to contain his laughter. 'What do you mean?'

'Don't get smart with me. We've been doing laps!'

'No we haven't.'

'We have! We were just here!'

'No we weren't.'

Alex pointed at the sign. 'That says D section, level nine!'

'All the corridors look the same to newbies. That's why you're always getting lost.'

'Is that so?' Alex plucked a hair and tucked it behind the corner of the sign. 'If I see that again, you'll be wearing this briefcase on your head.'

'If you do that every time we pass a sign you'll be as bald as a space helmet.' Hal led the way upstairs, and as they emerged on the long corridor once again, he was tempted to try for yet another lap. Unfortunately Alex had noticed his little ruse, and he suspected she wasn't kidding about hitting him with the briefcase.

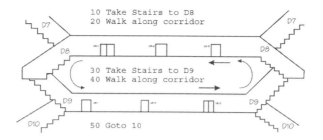

```
10 Take Stairs to D8
20 Walk along corridor

30 Take Stairs to D9
40 Walk along corridor

50 Goto 10
```

They were halfway along when Hal stopped. They'd just passed one of the many storage cupboards, and it had given him an idea. 'Listen, you know that briefcase?'

'I haven't exactly forgotten it,' Alex stopped, out of breath.

＊

'Why don't we stash it?'

Alex hesitated, clearly tempted. 'Where?'

Hal pointed to the storage cupboard. 'Nobody will find it in there.'

'I don't think I should. Dad trusted me with it.'

'He didn't know you'd have to carry it all over the place.' Hal opened the door, revealing a cupboard crammed with spare parts. The shelves were overflowing with racks of circuit boards and electronic components, and there were drums of cable stacked waist-high on the floor. 'Nobody's been in here for ages. It'll be safe enough.'

'All right, but if it goes missing –'

'It'll be fine,' said Hal firmly. He held the door open, and was about to follow Alex inside when she stopped him.

'You wait here. I don't want you to see where I'm hiding it.'

Hal shrugged. If she didn't trust him that was her problem.

Alex closed the door, and there was a lot of clattering and rustling. Then . . . *whoosh!*

Hal frowned. 'Alex? Are you there?'

'All done,' said Alex, opening the door and dusting off her hands.

'Where did you put it?'

'Like I'd tell you that!'

Hal shrugged. The hissing noise must have come from another deck. Odd sounds were common aboard the Station, but in that it was a bit like a spaceship or an aeroplane: people only started to panic when all the noises stopped. 'Come on, let's go.'

Alex hesitated. 'Are you sure the briefcase will be all right? I'll get in real trouble if –'

'Will you stop fussing?' demanded Hal. 'It's perfectly safe. Nobody knows where it is.'

As it turns out, he was even more accurate than he realised.

6

Tag!

Alex moved a lot faster without the briefcase, and they reached the recreation room in no time. Hal threw open the doors to reveal a spacious lounge with comfy chairs and glowing arcade machines, and he waited for Alex's thrilled reaction.

'Is that it?' Alex stared at the arcade games in disbelief. 'They're ancient!'

'I should have known you'd complain!' snapped Hal. He was about to slam the doors shut when Alex stopped him.

'All right, I'll play. It's not like there's anything else to do around here.' They entered the room, and she examined the controls on the nearest machine. 'Do people get burnt?'

'What do you mean?'

'When the steam comes out.'

Hal rolled his eyes.

'So how does it work?'

Hal picked up a helmet and showed her the projector screens and speakers fitted inside. When she was happy he demonstrated the joystick fixed to the front of each machine.

'I push that thing to move around?' asked Alex.

Hal smiled to himself. A total beginner!

'And the red switch on the front?'

'What do you think? That's the fire button!'

'Great. Let's go.'

'First to five wins the match,' declared Hal.

'Do these machines really count that high?'

They donned the helmets and Hal took hold of the controls. His display showed a darkened warehouse packed with large crates and walkways. The idea was to sneak around and tag the other player, and with a noob like Alex, Hal reckoned he'd win in ten seconds flat.

BUZZ!

'One nil,' said Alex.

'Hey! I wasn't ready!' protested Hal.

'Tell that to the scoring computer.'

Hal's eyes narrowed. So that's how it was! He forgot the rec room and immersed himself in the game, listening for stealthy footsteps as he crept between the towering stacks of crates. He held his gun at the ready, moving the laser dot from side to side as he tried to spot the enemy.

CRASH!

Hal almost jumped out of his shoes as a crate smashed into the ground right behind him. He stared at the shattered timbers, and realised someone had pushed it from the stack. Oh no . . . Alex was above him, on top of the stacks! His display whirled as he looked up, but he was much too late.

BUZZ!

'Two nil,' said Alex cheerfully.

Hal muttered under his breath. Nobody told him you could push the crates around! And if that was allowed, why not bring the whole building down on your enemy? Now there was an idea! He ran to the nearest wall and tried shooting out the supporting beams.

BUZZ!

'That's three,' said Alex. 'Do you want to play best of seven instead?'

'No!' Hal hunched over the controls, focusing on the screen as though his life depended on it. He was not going to lose at his favourite game. Keeping his eyes peeled, he crouched between two crates and turned the volume as high as it would go, listening for the soft footsteps that would pinpoint Alex.

Scrape, scrape.

Hal frowned. What was that?

Scrape.

Hal spun round, but all he could see was the wall of crates. Above him were more crates, stacked high, and far overhead was the roof.

Scrape . . . scrape.

Hal backed away slowly, puzzled by the noise. Then he saw a glint from one of the crates, and he realised it was Alex's gun poking through a hole. She'd climbed right inside and was pushing the hollow crate along like a battle tank!

BUZZ!

'Four nil,' said Alex. 'One more and you're toast.'

Hal ripped the helmet off. 'That's it! I'm not playing against a lousy cheat.'

'Sore loser.'

'Cheat!'

'If it was cheating the game wouldn't let me do it. Anyway, you'd have used the same trick if you knew about it.'

Hal knew she was right, but he still wasn't happy. This was his game, and she should be playing it properly! When he fought his friends they just ran around in circles while he tagged them. They didn't hide inside boxes, throw crates . . . or beat him!

'Come on, one more go,' said Alex. 'I don't really think you're a loser.'

Mollified, Hal donned the helmet again. This time he lasted a whole minute before Alex ran up the wall, back-flipped over his head and tagged him in the rear with her gun.

BUZZ!

'You lose,' said Alex. 'Want another match?'

Hal frowned. He enjoyed the game when he was winning, but it wasn't the same when someone used you for target practice. No wonder Stinky got tired of it. 'No, I've had enough.'

'Suit yourself, coward.'

'I am not!'

'Cluck, cluck, cluck . . . . chickeeeen!'

Hal saw red. 'I can beat you at this silly game any time!'

'Prove it!'

The scores reset to zero and Hal gripped the

controls, a determined look on his face. Once inside the warehouse he ran to the nearest crate and worked out how to get inside. He made a hole with his gun, then peered out.

Scrape, scrape.

This time he recognised the sound. Alex was inside another crate, creeping up on him! Very slowly he turned to watch, and that's when he saw her. She was sliding between two rows, moving her tagger in a small figure of eight as she tried to pick up his trail.

Scrape.

Hal held his breath as he turned his crate. Had she heard? No! She was still moving! Hal sighted along the stubby barrel, placed the laser dot right in the middle of Alex's crate, and pulled the trigger.

BUZZ!

Hal grinned. 'One nil to me.'

'Not bad, young Hal. The master approves!'

Flush with confidence, Hal ran into the dingy warehouse to score another point. He'd barely cleared the door when . . .

BUZZ!

'Yesss! Score one to Alex the mighty warrior.'

Hal sighed. She'd been waiting just inside the door with her back to the wall.

'Let's try a new playing field,' said Alex.

Hal blinked. He was standing in a lush forest, with boulders and streams replacing crates and sewage pipes. There were birds in the trees, fluttering from branch to branch, and sunlight shone between the leaves. It was the most beautiful thing he'd ever seen, and all he could do was stand there, entranced. Of course, he'd seen pictures of forests before, but this was different. This was just like being there.

BUZZ!

'Two-one!' Alex laughed. 'The game would last longer if you ran around a bit.'

'Is this what your planet looks like?'

'Some of it. Why?'

'It's . . . '

'Better than a mouldy old tin can in space?'

Hal frowned. 'Not better. Different.'

'Are we playing or what?'

Hal took up the controls but his heart wasn't in it. He didn't want to run around playing tag, he wanted to climb a tree, float sticks down the stream and enjoy the sunlight on his face.

A few minutes later the score was five to one, and Hal took off his helmet in silence. He looked around the rec room and decided it didn't look bright and welcoming any more. No, it looked sterile and artificial.

'No cheering for the winner?'

Hal shrugged. 'Congratulations.'

'You gave up, didn't you?'

'Yeah.' Hal frowned. 'I can't believe you learnt to play so quickly.'

'I've been playing these games for years.' Alex grinned. 'My dad owns the company that makes them.'

7

The AutoChef

'You already knew how to play?' Hal was really annoyed. 'You pretended you didn't! You asked me to show you how the controls worked!'

'My dad calls it mental conditioning. First you put people off their guard . . .'

'. . . And then you shoot them in the back,' finished Hal. 'Nice.'

'He's a businessman. It's what they do.' Alex gestured at another machine. 'Do you want to try that one?'

'No, let's get a snack.'

'I thought you didn't have restaurants?'

'We don't. We have something much better.' Hal led her across the rec room to an alcove, which contained a gleaming black cabinet covered with pictures of delicious food. There were pastries and sausage rolls and salads, as well as a sumptuous cake with cherries on top. 'This is the AutoChef,' said Hal. 'You tell it what you want, and it serves it up in seconds.'

'Really? Will you show me how it works?'

Hal wondered whether Alex was pretending again, but she sounded genuinely interested. 'Okay. Watch this.' He addressed the machine, speaking very clearly. 'I want a ham sandwich.'

'Order accepted,' said the AutoChef curtly. It rumbled and growled, and then . . . whizz! Zoom! Two slices of bread shot out of the dispenser and sailed halfway across the rec room before skidding to a halt, butter side down.

Chack! Chack! CHACK! went the machine, as it tossed slices of ham into the dispenser. Then, with a loud squir-ir-irt!, it spat a cupful of yellowy-brown mustard all over the ham. Hal scraped the bread clean and built a sandwich with the dripping ham.

'Yum, that looks great,' said Alex, trying not to laugh. 'I wish I had a machine like that.'

'I don't know what's wrong with it,' muttered Hal. 'It doesn't usually do that.'

'Can I try?'

'Sure, but don't order stew or you might get p–'

'Yes, I get the picture.' Alex turned to the machine. 'Hello AutoChef. Please may I have a garden salad with shaved ham, olives and two slices of bread?'

41

Hal stared in horror. Was she mad? That lot would have them knee deep in goop!

'Order accepted.' The machine hissed and groaned, and Hal backed away. He was expecting a tidal wave at the very least.

'Oh, I nearly forgot,' continued Alex. 'Acknowledge supervisor code nine-six-two.'

'Code acknowledged.' The hissing and growling turned into an even hum, and Hal was stunned when the machine delivered Alex's order. It was arranged on a real plate, and everything was perfect! 'How did you do that?' he demanded, staring at the delicious food.

'It doesn't hurt to say please and thank you.' Alex patted the AutoChef. 'Machines have feelings too, you know.'

'What about that supervisor code?'

'Oh, that. Well, my dad's company makes these machines too, and the code tells them when they're serving VIPs.'

Hal felt a flash of annoyance. Alex had shown him up again! Then he realised what the supervisor code meant. 'Hey, does that mean I can get real food out of the AutoChef too?' Hal could just imagine the scene: Get all his classmates there and show off with some incredible dishes. 'Does it do real cake?'

Alex dashed his hopes. 'Sorry, but it only works with a few recognised voices. And as for a computer giving you cake ... get real!' She saw his downcast expression, and relented. 'Here, you can have my lunch. I'll get something else.'

Wide-eyed, Hal took the tray and enjoyed the best lunch ever. Crisp lettuce, fresh tomatoes, tangy olives and ham! They weren't real meat and vegetables, of course. His dad once explained how everything the AutoChef served was assembled from a kind of raw goop, blending molecules to simulate real food. When the goop ran out there was no more food, which is why you never ordered more than you could eat.

Real or not, the food still tasted amazing to Hal.

Alex ordered another lunch, but she hadn't finished with the machine yet. 'I'd also like a strawberry thickshake, two straws, and one of those cakes with the chocolate stuff on top.'

The machine made a horrible gargling sound. 'Error C-22.'

'You've broken it!' said Hal in alarm.

'Relax. It's just run out of material.'

Hal frowned. He fancied dessert, and didn't see why they shouldn't have any. 'I know where we can go next.'

'You do?'

'They're preparing a special lunch for your dad. Let's sneak into the kitchens and help ourselves!'

❖

'Oh no you don't, my lad. Out! Out! OUT!'

Hal took one look at the angry-looking chef and scarpered. Once he'd retreated to a safe distance he paused to catch his breath.

'Wow, you're really popular around here,' said Alex. 'It's like one big happy family.'

'At least my mum didn't run away,' snapped Hal. Then he realised what he'd said. 'I'm sorry, I–'

'Leave it.'

They stood near the entrance, watching the bustle as chefs put the finishing touches to a vast array of different foods. 'Maybe we could help carry,' said Hal, licking his lips.

'Yeah, like they're going to trust you.'

'Do you think your dad will eat it all?'

'You bet.'

Hal frowned. For his last birthday they'd had a stale sponge with fake cream, and at the time it was one of the best things he'd ever tasted. Now he was looking at strawberry tarts, scones with jam and dollops of fresh cream, chocolate cake with thick icing and gooey filling, and currant buns spread with more butter than he'd seen in his entire life. At that moment Hal would have given up his precious watch for any one of the treats on display.

Beep beep! 'Mind your backs!'

There was a loud whirr, and Hal jumped aside as a powered trolley shot into the kitchens. It was almost as big as the doorway, and it moved on huge rubber wheels.

'Where have you been?' shouted one of the chefs. 'These cakes ain't going to deliver themselves!'

The trolley apologised. 'I had to stop for a recharge. All this extra activity drained my batteries.'

The chef beckoned to her staff. 'You lot. Get this trolley loaded. Now!'

Hal watched the bustle with a thoughtful look on

his face. The trolley had a tablecloth draped over the top, and it hung almost to the floor. The kitchen hands were putting cakes on the top shelf, and as he watched them Hal got the beginnings of an idea. He glanced down the corridor to the next doorway, then nudged Alex. 'Come on. Follow me.'

'I thought you wanted cake?'

'I do, and I know how to get some.'

The kitchen doors closed behind them, and Hal hurried down the access tunnel to the second pair of doors. 'You stand that side,' he said. 'Get ready to watch the master in action.'

Moments later the trolley zoomed out of the kitchen, cakes and jellies shivering and jiggling on top.

Beep beep! 'Stand aside please!'

The doors began to open, and Hal quickly pressed the close button.

Screeeeeeech!

The trolley slid to a halt in a cloud of tyre smoke, plates of food skidding along the top shelf. Fortunately there was a rail, else the contents would have splatted into the doors. Hal grinned triumphantly at Alex, and was just about to choose a sticky cake when the kitchen doors started to open. Someone was coming! They were trapped!

'Get inside!' hissed Alex.

Hal saw Alex climbing into the trolley, and he lifted the tablecloth and scrambled in after her.

'Wait!' shouted a female voice. There was a patter of footsteps, and Hal realised they'd been spotted.

'Watch the master in action?' hissed Alex. 'Watch the master get caught, you mean!'

There was barely enough room for the two of them, and they sat facing each other with their arms clasped around their knees. It was very dark, but Hal could still see Alex's amused expression. It was all a big joke to her, but what sort of punishment could he expect *this* time?

8

Carrie

The footsteps halted right next to the trolley, and then . . . 'Can you return to the kitchen, please? We've not finished loading.'

The trolley obeyed, reversing direction and slowly whirring back to the kitchen. Hal breathed a sigh of relief. They hadn't been spotted after all! Of course, that would soon change if someone tried to use the lower shelf.

The trolley stopped, and someone tutted as they straightened the plates on top.

'Millie, are you done yet?' demanded the chef.

'Last two,' said a voice . . . presumably Millie.

'Don't cram them so. Use the lower shelf.'

Hal held his breath as the tablecloth was lifted. A plate full of jam doughnuts was pushed in, and Hal quickly moved his foot. He was still expecting a shout of discovery when the tablecloth fell back into place.

'Anything else, chef?' asked Millie.

'No, that's everything. Trolley, to the meeting room. And not so fast, mind!'

The engine groaned, but the trolley didn't move.

'Trolley, to the meeting room!'

'Unable to comply,' said the trolley. 'Total weight exceeds safety limits.'

'Nonsense! Millie, give that thing a push.'

The trolley turned slowly towards the exit, while Millie huffed and puffed and complained about the chef's cooking.

'What was that?' demanded the chef. 'What did you say about my rock cakes?'

'They're too heavy,' grumbled Millie. 'This trolley weighs a ton!'

'Come here and say that!' growled the chef.

Millie didn't do anything of the sort. Instead she gave the trolley a big shove to get it moving, and the plate of doughnuts slid along the shelf and stopped next to Hal's hand. One of the jam doughnuts actually came to rest against his fingers, and he could feel the sticky wetness. If he picked it up he could open his mouth and ... But no. When someone eventually discovered Hal and Alex hiding in the trolley, they'd notice the missing doughnut and Hal would be in more trouble than ever.

◆

Hal and Alex held on tight as the trolley rumbled along the corridor. It was very quiet, with only the whirr of the motor and the rattle of crockery to break the silence.

They stared at each other in the darkness. The trolley was going to the meeting, and that was in A-section. If they were discovered sneaking into the top-secret labs, Hal suspected he wouldn't just be confined to quarters. They'd banish him from the Space Station!

Ten minutes later Hal had forgotten all about A-section, and nothing was further from his mind than sticky doughnuts. He couldn't believe how much the trolley swayed on its rubber wheels, and the motion was making him seasick.

'If you want to get off, just say the word.'

Hal heard the electronic voice, and with a shock he realised the trolley was talking to him. 'You know we're here?'

'Of course.' The trolley chuckled. 'Even chef's rock cakes aren't that heavy.'

'Thanks for not telling. Back in the kitchen, I mean.'

'We're all young once.' The trolley hesitated. 'Why don't we introduce ourselves?'

'I'm Hal and this is Alex. And you?'

'My name is Carrie.'

'Can you stop before we get to A-Section?'

'Sure. I'll let you know when the coast is clear.'

They rolled on for another minute or two, then came to a halt. 'This should do,' said Carrie. 'There's nobody around, but I'd get out fast if I were you.'

Hal leapt out, holding up the tablecloth so Alex could follow. He glanced at the nearby sign to get his bearings, then groaned. 'Quick, back in the trolley!'

Too late! When they turned to hide they discovered Carrie had already moved off, and the speeding trolley disappeared around the corner with a final beep! beep!

There was a whirr behind them, and Hal heard a familiar electronic voice. 'What are you doing here, Hal Junior? I thought you were confined to your cabin!'

They turned to see a bright red robot with yellow stripes. It had a big grey screen where its face should have been, and there were two dozen assorted eyes staring at Hal.

'Is that a security bot?' whispered Alex fearfully.

'No, much worse.' Hal sighed. 'It's Teacher.'

— 9 —

Spring

'Well, Hal Junior?' said Teacher. 'Explain your presence!'

Hal told him about Alex and the VIP, and while he was talking Teacher turned several eyes on the girl. 'Welcome to the Space Station, Alex. I trust Hal isn't getting you into trouble?'

'No, not at all.'

'I find that surprising.' Teacher frowned at Hal. 'This young man can be irresponsible and unreliable at times. Starting a fire aboard the Space Station! What were you thinking?'

'It was an experiment,' said Hal. 'You're always telling me to light up my grades.'

'Hmph.' Teacher turned a couple more eyes on them both. 'Now you're here, why don't you help with spring cleaning?'

Cleaning? Hal would rather have gone for a space

walk without a suit! Then he frowned. As far as he knew Teacher ran on batteries, not springs.

Teacher noticed his puzzled look and launched into an explanation. 'As you know, many planets experience hot and cold seasons called Summer and Winter. After Summer comes Autumn, also known as Fall or Harvest, and after Winter you get Spring, which is only known as Spring.'

'So why are you doing spring cleaning when we don't have seasons?'

'It's a tradition. Once a year we have a big tidy-up before the end of term.'

'I don't remember any tidy-ups.'

Teacher frowned. 'No, I always seem to get a sick note from your parents. Written, I must say, in a rather ungrammatical fashion.'

Hal blushed, and quickly changed the subject. 'So why do we have years aboard the Space Station when we don't orbit a star?'

'The same reason we have days and nights. To remain in sync with the rest of the galaxy. Now, please follow me. I'm sure I can find something for you to do.'

Hal and Alex exchanged a glance, but there was no escape. They entered the classroom behind Teacher and stopped to take in the chaos. Desks and chairs had been pushed out to the walls and two dozen children were emptying all the cupboards onto the floor, stirring the contents around and piling them up at random. At least, that's what it looked like to Hal, whose own 'cleaning' sessions ran along similar lines.

'No, no, no!' Teacher darted away to supervise, swerving on his rubber wheels to avoid the children. 'Harold, I said to place those workbooks in a neat pile! Marcia, do NOT stand on the geometry shapes to reach the upper shelves. Tim, if you break one more beaker . . . '

Hal eyed the crowd, trying to pick out his best friend, but he was nowhere to be seen. 'Teacher, where's Stinky?'

'Master Binn is running an errand for me.' One of Teacher's eyes turned to the door. 'Unless I'm mistaken, that's him now.'

Stinky entered the classroom, looking worried. His face was red from running, and his hair - usually so tidy - was sticking out all over the place. With his singed eyebrows and flushed face he looked like a sunburned kiwi fruit, and it was all Hal could do not to laugh.

'Master Binn, were you successful?'

'I'm sorry Teacher. They wouldn't let me have any.'

'That's a pity.'

'You won't . . . mark me down, will you?'

'Master Binn, this is spring cleaning, not final exams. Your grades are safe.'

Hal rolled his eyes. His friend's biggest nightmare was getting a B in something, even though he had a string of A's reaching all the way back to kindy. 'Hey, Stinky! I want you to meet someone. This is Alex.'

Stinky met the girl's level gaze for a second, then turned an even brighter shade of red. 'N-nice to meet you,' he stammered.

'What happened to your eyebrows?' asked Alex.

'Never mind that,' said Hal quickly. 'What did Teacher send you off for? Maybe Alex and me can help.'

Teacher heard him, and zoomed across the room. 'Hal Junior! I'm sure you meant *I* can help.'

'How can you? You're busy here.'

'I meant *you* could help, not me.'

'That's exactly what I said!'

One of Teacher's eyes flickered. 'You said me.'

'No, I said *Alex* and me. Anyway, you're busy.'

Several of Teacher's eyes bounced along the bottom of his face. 'It's Alex and *I*. Alex and *I*!'

Alex looked doubtful. 'I'd rather stay with Hal,' she said. 'I don't really know you very well.'

'I– I– I–' Teacher's eyes bounced around like a

handful of glass marbles falling downstairs, some of them going all the way round his head before reappearing the other side.

'We just need some boxes,' said Stinky quickly, before Teacher crashed completely.

'Don't worry,' said Hal, patting him on the shoulder. 'Alex and me will get them for you.'

'I, not me,' muttered Teacher. 'I. Eye. Aye aye.'

Stinky gave Hal a printed card.

'What's that?'

'Permission slip. You'll need it to get the boxes.'

'It didn't do you any good.' Hal looked closer. 'Anyway, it's got your name all over it.'

'Get another from Teacher.'

Hal eyed the robot doubtfully. Teacher's eyes were still ping-ponging all over his face, and the last time that happened the techs had taken two hours to reboot him. Then Hal had a thought, and a slow smile spread across his face. With a permission slip he could roam the entire Space Station!

There was a thud nearby as a pile of workbooks toppled over, and Teacher snapped out of his loop instantly. 'Harold, will you please be careful! And Marcia, get your foot off that equipment. Don't you know how fragile it is?'

'Can I get a permission slip?' asked Hal, before

Teacher could zoom away to rescue his precious equipment.

'Very well. Where do you need to go?'

'I don't know yet.'

'You'll have to be more specific.'

'The lower levels,' said Hal. He hadn't been right to the bottom of the Space Station before, and now was his chance.

Teacher paused. 'I don't think I can –'

'Oh, go on! We can't get boxes anywhere else, and Alex is sensible. She's a . . . ' Hal tried to remember some of the things his parents wanted him to be. 'She's a good influence, and she's prompt, and she brushes her hair and does all her homework.'

'Very well. You make a good point.' Teacher clicked his fingers and a printed card popped out the palm of his hand. 'It's valid for one hour. Please return with the boxes as soon as you can.'

— 10 —

Order! Order!

As they left the classroom Alex plucked the permission card from Hal's fingers. 'I'll be in charge.'

'Says who?'

'Teacher said you're irresponsible, unreliable and un– un–'

'Unable to take orders from you,' finished Hal.

'Why don't we go back inside and ask Teacher which of us is leader?'

Alex went to open the classroom door, but Hal put his hand over the controls. Imagine the embarrassment if Teacher made him second-in-command! 'Let's share the power between us.'

'Like that's going to work.'

'No, it will. We'll take it in turns to give orders. One for you, one for me.'

'Fine, but I'm going first.'

Hal shrugged. If he didn't like the orders he'd ignore them . . . just like he always did.

'My first order is this: I order you not to give me any silly orders. Now it's your turn.'

'I order you not to speak for the rest of my life.'

'That'll be ten seconds from now if you keep this up.' Alex thought for a moment. 'I order you to be sensible.'

'I order you a ham sandwich.'

'Hal Junior! Quit messing around!'

'I order you not to give me any more orders,' said Hal quickly. 'And I order you not to tell Teacher on me.'

'Oh, this is stupid!' cried Alex. 'We're fetching some mouldy old boxes, not leading an expedition to the centre of the Galaxy. Who cares which of us is in charge?'

'Of course, if we don't bring back any boxes the person in charge is going to get the blame.'

Alex pursed her lips. 'I think you should be leader.'

'No, you do it.'

'Your Teacher expects you to fail. It sounds like you're always getting in trouble.' Alex crossed her arms. 'I order you to take charge.'

'About time.' Hal grabbed the permission slip. 'Now quit talking and follow me.'

Looking a bit dazed, Alex fell in behind Hal as they made their way to the lift.

'So where are you getting these boxes?' she asked, after a moment or two. 'Your friend Stinky didn't think there were any.'

Hal took a deep breath, then revealed his master plan. 'Stinky didn't go to the recycling centre, did he?'

'The what?'

'It's like a huge rubbish dump at the bottom of the Space Station. Everything we throw away ends up there.'

'Oh, wonderful. First school and now the local tip. You really know how to show someone the sights, you do.'

Hal frowned. 'Don't you understand? The recycling centre is off-limits! We're not allowed there!'

'Why not?'

'Dangerous, maybe. Some of the kids think there's a space monster.'

'So speaks the straight-A student.' Alex laughed. 'Anyone with half a brain knows space monsters don't exist.'

Hal's eyes narrowed. 'Are you saying I'm dumb?'

'No, but I don't think you try very hard.'

'I don't see the point! All that math and writing

and stuff . . . what use is that to me? I'm going to be a space pilot!'

Alex raised one eyebrow. 'Next time you're sitting at a terminal, look up navigation. I think you'll be surprised.'

They walked in silence while Hal considered her words. Did you really need to study sums to fly a spaceship? How could that be right?

They were only halfway along the corridor when Hal heard a whirr behind them. He turned around, half-expecting to see Teacher pursuing him with new instructions, but instead he saw Carrie. The motorised trolley was bearing down on them with a load of empty dishes piled on top. Hal frowned at this: Alex's greedy dad *had* eaten all the food!

Beep beep! 'Mind your backs!'

'Hey, Carrie. Stop!'

'I can't. I'm in a hurry.'

'So are we,' said Hal quickly. 'Teacher sent us on an important errand, and our pass is only valid for one hour.'

The trolley came to a halt. 'Very well, but you mustn't delay me.'

'We won't!' Hal raised the tablecloth so Alex could get inside, and when they were both settled he rapped his knuckles on the floor. 'Let's go.'

The trolley moved off with a jerk, and once they were speeding along Carrie asked where they were going.

'To the recycling centre,' said Hal.

Screech! Hal and Alex were almost thrown out as the trolley came to a shuddering halt. 'Out, both of you.'

'But –'

'Out!' Carrie's voice was angry. 'You'll never get me near that place. Never!'

'Just to the lift, then? We have to fetch something, I swear!'

'We'd all like something back from the recycling centre,' said Carrie. 'When I started working in the kitchens there was another trolley just like me. He was pretty old, Paul was, and he needed a few repairs. Just simple things like a new back wheel and a bit of polish, but they recycled him instead.' Carrie shuddered. 'He was gone, just like that! Turned into nuts and bolts.'

'I'm sorry.'

Carrie's voice softened. 'At night, when the kitchens were closed, Paul used to sing for us. It was . . . nice.'

There was a lengthy silence.

'All right,' said Carrie at last. 'I'll take you to the lift, but not one metre further. Is that clear?'

'Thanks Carrie.' As the trolley picked up speed Hal glanced at Alex. So far she'd met a surly guard, an angry chef, a Teacher who kept crashing and now a trolley whose best friend was nuts. So much for staying out of trouble!

Lower Levels

Carrie got slower and slower the closer they got to the main lift, and once they were in sight of the doors the trolley came to a shuddering halt. 'That's it. I'm not going a centimetre further.'

Hal and Alex climbed out, and Carrie sped away before they could say thanks.

'The recycling centre must be pretty dangerous,' said Alex.

'Bring it on,' said Hal, as he pressed the call button.

'Can't you think of somewhere else to get these boxes?'

'Sure. We can plant some trees, wait around for them to grow, then slice them real thin and fold the sheets into cubes. It won't take more than ten or fifteen years, plus a hundred years of my water ration.'

'There's no need to be sarcastic.'

The lift arrived and the doors parted with a whoosh. Hal motioned Alex inside, then jammed his thumb on the lowest button. The doors closed and the lift dropped like a stone.

'Bet you get into trouble,' said Alex.

That was one bet Hal wasn't willing to take. 'This is an official mission. We can go anywhere we want and take anything we like.'

'I don't suppose you got these carte-blanche orders in writing?'

'Carty what?'

'Carte blanche. It means full power to do anything you want.'

'Why didn't you say that instead?' complained Hal.

'I was trying to educate you.'

'That's Teacher's job.'

'If we get caught I'm dobbing,' said Alex.

'You would too. You're such a feeb.'

'Am not.'

'Are so!'

Alex turned her back on him and Hal ground his teeth in silence. As they dropped further and further the elevator began to squeak and rattle in its tracks, as though it rarely came down this far.

Would it break free and plunge all the way to the bottom?

But no, it finally came to a halt, and the doors grated open to reveal a dark, forbidding corridor. Hal and Alex stood side by side, each waiting for the other to take the first step.

'What was that you said about a space monster?' asked Alex at last.

Hal wished he'd never mentioned it. He'd been trying to forget the stories all the way down. The ones about the monster at the very bottom of the space station. The monster which ate all the junk and chewed up anyone who fell down the recycling chute. The monster which might be hiding just around the corner, ready to pounce.

'Why don't we sneak into A-section instead?' suggested Alex, her voice a little uneven. 'They might have boxes in the labs.'

Hal was tempted, but then he remembered his watch. After his last adventure it had been engraved with 'Hal Junior, Saviour of Space Station Oberon', and they didn't hand those out to people afraid of a silly old space monster. 'Come on, it'll be fine.'

'You're in charge. You should go first.'

'Just watch me. I'm not afraid.' Nevertheless Hal didn't exactly hurry out of the elevator, and he'd only taken a dozen faltering steps when there was a flash of light and a loud *BUZZ-CRACKLE!* directly overhead. He suppressed a startled squeak and almost bolted for safety. Then he realised it was just an automatic light coming on. Dim and dusty, the fitting gave out barely enough light to see by, and Hal kept moving until he reached the end of the corridor.

'Can you see anything?' hissed Alex, as Hal peered around the corner.

'Oh wow!' breathed Hal. 'It's incredible!'

'What is?'

'Come and look!'

Reluctantly, Alex left the elevator. When she reached the corner she peered round and saw . . . 'You cheat! It's just another corridor!'

'Shh!' Hal put a finger to his lips. 'The monster might hear you!'

'If you're going to play silly games I'm leaving.'

'Oh come on. Maybe there's something interesting round the next corner.'

Hal set off along the corridor with Alex grumbling in his wake. Before long they reached a big pair of doors. The paint was peeling and the panels had streaks of rust running down them, and judging from the layer of dirt on the floor nobody had been this way for quite some time. Hal reached for the control panel, but before he could press the button Alex grabbed his arm. 'Shouldn't we knock or something?'

'On that?' Hal eyed the slab of metal. 'I could bang on that until my knuckles broke, and they still wouldn't hear me on the other side.' He shook his arm free and thumped his fist on the door controller. There was an agonising groan as the motor whirred into life, and then the doors began to open with a horrible grating sound.

The noise was incredible, and even though Hal covered his ears he could still feel the groaning through the soles of his shoes. As the doors opened a foul-smelling wind blew out, ruffling their hair. Hal wrinkled his nose and hoped the stink wouldn't spread through the entire station.

'Now youb dub id,' said Alex, who was holding her nose. 'Deyr godda smer dad all over da dadion.'

The doors stopped moving and Hal risked a quick look inside. He knew there was a main shaft down the centre of the Space Station, with several smaller chutes connecting various living areas, but he hadn't realised the inhabitants generated this much rubbish. Instead of the large room he'd been expecting there was a gigantic, poorly-lit cavern, so big he couldn't make out the far wall. This was a new experience for Hal, who'd grown up with corridors and confined spaces.

He gazed around and discovered the floor was covered in junk piles, from little ones right up to huge mountains. The biggest were right underneath a row of holes in the ceiling, which Hal realised were the bases of the recycling shafts. These huge square openings gaped like giant silver mouths, and one of them disgorged a stream of rubbish onto the top of a pile while they were standing there watching. Steam rose from the fresh junk in waves, adding to the foggy atmosphere.

'Yuck,' said Alex. 'That's gross!'

Hal didn't think it was gross at all. Just imagine what treasures they might find in this vast, unexplored cavern! Imagine the fun they could have here! There was enough room to build a go-kart and race between the piles of rubbish, space to build a clubhouse and run a secret society, and great stacks of building materials just lying around waiting to be used.

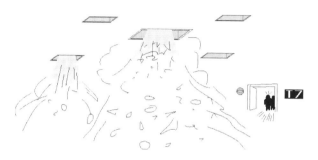

Hal crossed to a big pile of wall panels and ran his hand over the smooth plastic. Half a dozen of these would make a great clubhouse, and if he could find some paint they could have a big sign above the door. He was just deciding whether to call the group the 'Junior Outlaws' or 'Hal's Heroes' when Alex piped up.

'Let's grab some boxes and get out of here.'

'No, we'll look around a bit first.'

'But –'

'Who's in charge, you or me?' Hal scanned the recycling centre from end to end, peering through the murk as he tried to spot any workers, guards or automated defence turrets with dual blasters and laser-guided gunsights. Fortunately there was nothing of the kind, but in the distance he could see a rickety-looking shed nestled between a discarded exhaust cone and a pile of frayed spacesuits. The door was closed but the window was lit from within, and at that moment he spotted movement inside. 'Down!' he hissed.

They both dropped to the floor, then raised their heads to see whether they'd been spotted. Fortunately the shadow was still moving behind the window.

'Who is it?' hissed Alex.

'I don't know. Someone who works here.'

'So why are we hiding?' whispered Alex. 'You have permission, don't you?'

Hal didn't answer. He pointed away from the office, and together they crawled into the recycling centre, keeping low so as not to be spotted.

— 12 —

Attack the Summit!

They rounded a big pile of junk on hands and knees, clambering to their feet as soon as they were shielded from the office. They were approaching the middle of the recycling centre now, and there was a low-pitched hum in the air. There was something else too . . . a deep *THUD!* every so often, which shook the floor under their feet.

'Fee fie –' began Alex.

'That's not funny,' muttered Hal. Years ago his parents had told him the story of Jack and the Space Elevator, and the sound of the giant robot's footsteps as it chased Jack haunted Hal's nightmares for years. He wasn't that keen on greens either, especially beans.

They reached a large junk pile, and Hal stopped to look at the top.

'Don't tell me you're going to climb it,' said Alex.

Hal hadn't been planning anything of the sort, but he couldn't resist a challenge. 'Of course I am.'

'Why?'

'Because it's there,' said Hal firmly. He'd heard the line in a mountaineering documentary Teacher had shown the class a few months earlier. At the time Hal felt cheated, because there was no chance he'd ever climb a mountain, and he wondered whether Teacher was going to follow up the first documentary with others on scuba diving, bike riding and skiing.

Anyway, the documentary had been pretty cool in the end. *Attack the Summit!* was the name, and the climbers had been dressed in boots and goggles and thick orange jackets, and their equipment included a T-shaped tool on a length of rope. The leader had swung the tool over her head, then flung it up the slope before pulling it tight and using it to haul herself up the icy slopes. After she tested the rope the rest of the team followed, until it was time to throw the tool once more.

Hal didn't need the goggles or the orange jackets, but one of those T-shaped tools and a length of climbing rope would be pretty useful. Unfortunately, aboard the Space Station he was more likely to find a pair of hover boots or a portable jet pack, and his live-action remake of

Attack the Summit! was likely to turn into *Rolling down the mountain.*

He was still working out the easiest way to the top of the pile when Alex spoke up.

'If you're going to climb something, why not make it a real challenge?'

'What do you mean?'

Alex jerked her thumb towards the largest pile of all. 'Bet you can't climb that one.'

Hal craned his neck back … and further back … and further back still, until he was finally looking at the top. It was shrouded in fog from a fresh load of garbage, and the towering mass reached almost to the distant ceiling. 'Sure I can.'

'Bet you can't.'

'I can!'

'If you make it right to the top I'll … I'll give you my watch!'

Hal stared. With a watch like that he'd be the envy of the entire station. Sure, the pile of junk was enormous, but what a prize! 'For real?'

'Of course,' said Alex coldly. 'I said it, didn't I?'

'Wait right here.' Hal strolled over to the pile and tested it with his foot. It was spongy and loose, but it wasn't too steep and he managed to climb the first few metres without any trouble. After that the going got harder, and he'd never have made it without a fantastic stroke of luck. First, his foot got caught in a loop of network cable, and then he spotted a heavy metal bar. The metal bar was bent into a J-shape, and it reminded him of the climbing tool the mountaineers had used. Within moments he'd freed the network cable and attached it to the long end of the J. Then he swung it overhead and threw it as hard as he could towards the top of the pile.

Unfortunately, he slipped as he threw, and he landed face down in the junk. The heavy metal bar hardly made it halfway to the top, and Hal was still recovering when he realised it had dislodged a load of plastic bags, broken furniture and battered air filters. The avalanche of junk rumbled towards him, and he barely had time to lie flat and cover his head. The slithering mess arrived with a rush, covering Hal from head to toe and burying him up to his neck. He poked his head up just as the heavy bar shot past, close enough to scrape his cheek, and then the network cord it was tied to nearly gave him a crew cut.

Hal rolled onto his back, winded and surprised by the near miss. He heard Alex calling to him, and he gave her a thumbs up. Then he staggered to his feet, retrieved the climbing tool and prepared to throw it again. This time he anchored his feet properly, and the metal bar hummed as he spun it round and round, faster and faster. He let go with a gigantic heave, and watched in satisfaction as the bar zoomed over the top of the pile. He pulled on the network cable to test it was secure, then started the slow climb to the top.

Hal soon discovered how hard it was to climb a steep slope, especially with his arms doing most of the work. His feet slipped and skidded on the loose junk, his muscles ached like mad, but metre by agonising metre he made his way towards the summit. So much for those adults with their orange jackets and goggles, he thought. He was doing the same thing with home-made equipment!

Hal's hands were sweaty on the thin network cable, and his fingers ached from holding it so tight. There was sweat in his eyes too, but he wasn't about to brush it away, not if it meant letting go of the rope.

Moments later Hal felt the pile shift under his feet. He froze until it settled, then continued even more carefully. He was a long way above the ground now, and the last thing he wanted was to tumble all the way to the bottom inside an avalanche of materials.

When Hal finally reached the top he dropped the network cable and struck a heroic pose: chest out, head back and one foot resting casually on a dented old bucket. It was a very proud moment, and he glanced down at Alex out of the corner of his eye, trying to gauge how impressed she was. She was standing with her arms crossed, a sour look on her face.

At that moment Hal heard a rumble overhead. He looked up and realised he was directly under the recycling chute, which was pointing down at him like the gaping mouth of a huge cannon. Several plastic wrappers fluttered down on him, and Hal abandoned the heroic pose and dived for safety, just as a fresh load of junk thundered out of the chute.

Dust and rubbish blew around like a mini tornado, and when it finally settled Hal sat up and started picking bits out of his hair. The foggy air cleared a little, and that's when he happened to look down far side of the enormous junk pile.

What he saw almost took his breath away.

— 13 —

Thud!

Laid out below was a huge machine, stretching the entire width of the recycling centre. At one end there was a pair of arms with gigantic hands, which were busy grabbing junk from the pile. As Hal watched, huge fingers plucked a rusty beam from a pile of junk, picking it up as though it weighed no more than a ration bar. It tried to put the beam onto a conveyor belt, but the metal was far too long and wouldn't fit. Hal wondered whether it would give up, but no! The second hand grabbed the loose end of the beam and . . . screeeaakk . . . they bent it in two! Hal gulped. Imagine if he'd rolled down the other side of the junk pile . . . those huge hands might have picked him up and squished him like a bug!

Thud!

The U-shaped beam landed on the conveyor belt,

which carried it towards a slab-sided box in the middle of the machine. The beam vanished and there was a loud grinding noise, as though someone had dropped a handful of gravel into a blender.

Something was happening on the other side of the box, and Hal stood up to get a better view. There was a smaller conveyor belt, full of glowing metal bars. A much smaller hand grabbed the bars one by one, throwing them neatly into a small red machine. There was an ear-splitting screeeee! as each bar vanished, and seconds later hundreds of shiny screws and nuts and bolts poured from a spout. These fell into containers, which were packed up and placed on another conveyor belt.

The process wasn't finished yet: even more arms grabbed the packaged goods from the conveyor belt, stacking them on a small black table. The table bowed under the weight, and Hal stared as it started to move. It wasn't a table at all, it was a motorised trolley! Then Hal saw something which made him gasp. The trolley was wobbling as it moved, and when he looked closer he noticed one of its wheel was bent. It was Carrie's friend Paul! He hadn't been recycled at all, he'd been put to work down here!

Even at this distance Hal could hear the squeak-squeak-squeak of Paul's damaged wheel, and he realised the trolley was being mistreated. He vowed to tell Carrie about her old friend, and he wondered whether a whole bunch of kitchen equipment would mount a daring midnight raid to get Paul back.

Hal turned his attention back to the machine, where the big hands were still busy. One had just dropped a fistful of broken wall panels onto the conveyor belt, and the machine hissed and spat as it converted them into plastic cubes. Then they went into a silver machine, which spat out brand new plates, cups and cutlery. Hal's eyes shone as he watched the entire operation. Just wait until he brought Stinky down for a look!

Then he remembered Alex . . . and his new watch.

A one Hal open sleigh

Hal now faced a new challenge: How was he going to climb down again? If it had been a pile of dirt he could have sat down and slid to the bottom, but the junk was much too lumpy and uneven for that. Then he spotted a buckled metal door from a locker, and it gave him an idea. He freed the door from the pile, laid it flat, and sat on it. He grabbed hold of the rusty door handle, and with his free hand he pushed off.

'Whooo-*hoooo!*' yelled Hal, as the makeshift toboggan took off down the slope. He was forced to hang on with all his strength as it gathered speed, and when it launched off a bundle of plastic pipes he was thrown high into the air. SLAM! went the buckled door as it landed again. OOF! went Hal, as he flopped down on top.

The makeshift toboggan finally reached the

bottom of the pile, where it skidded sideways and slowed to a halt. Hal stepped off at the last second, and he wished the kids from class had witnessed his incredible ride. He wanted to climb up for another go, until he saw Alex waiting impatiently nearby. She had her arms crossed, she was tapping her foot, and he realised he'd left her standing there for ages.

'I hope *you* enjoyed your holidays,' grumbled Alex, as soon as he was close.

'Come and see what I found.'

'Is it anything to do with rubbish?'

'Yeah, but it's still cool.'

'Nothing about rubbish is cool. Oh yeah, and this is yours.'

Hal felt something smooth in his hand, and when he looked down he realised it was Alex's watch. For a second he was tempted, but then he shook his head. 'I can't take it.'

'Sure you can. I'll buy another when I get home.'

Hal knew he couldn't keep it, but he'd pretend it was his until he figured out a way to give it back. Then he remembered the huge recycling machine. 'Do you want to see this amazing thing I found or not?'

'Not.'

'I bet you'll like it.'

'I won't.'

'I bet you will.' Hal held his hand up, showing Alex her own watch. 'If you like what I've found I'll give you this amazing space watch. It's even got a built-in torch.'

Alex's frown vanished, and she laughed. 'All right, I give in. Show me this amazing find.'

◆

Thud!

Screeeee!

Brrrrrrr!

Thud!

Hal gave Alex a running commentary as the huge recycling machine went through its paces. The arms grabbed junk, the tubes and conveyor belts extruded parts, and all the while Hal explained the various operations as though he'd invented the device himself.

'That is so cool!' exclaimed Alex, as an old table was turned into a stack of spacesuit visors.

Wordlessly, Hal slipped the watch off and pressed it into her hand. In return he got a grateful smile.

'Do you think it'll make cardboard boxes?' asked Alex, gesturing towards the machine.

Hal remembered their mission. 'What if we feed some old cardboard in?'

'I wouldn't get too close to the hands. Those fingers look pretty strong, and if they scooped you up . . .'

'Are you saying I look like rubbish?'

'You're not too bad . . . for a spacebug.'

'Thanks, earthworm.'

They made their way towards the machine, stopping just out of range of the huge hands. Hal decided to try an experiment, and he pulled a long metal tube out of the pile and waved it like a flagpole. Success! One of the hands plucked the pole out of his grasp, pinching and folding the tube before placing it onto the conveyor belt. Then both hands came back, hovering expectantly.

Grinning, Hal found an old door and stood it on end. He tried to lift it up but it was too heavy, until Alex helped. The hand took it between finger and thumb, and the door vanished into the machine. The other hand darted down to take a big piece of cardboard Alex was holding up, and when that disappeared into the machine it emerged as cardboard boxes.

'That's it, it's working!' cried Hal. 'Find more!'

They unearthed a whole lot of cardboard, and before long there was a stack of neatly folded boxes alongside the recycling machine. Then . . . disaster. Hal shouldered aside a battered old flight console, trying to reach a stash of cardboard underneath. One of the hands darted in and grabbed the entire console, but then Hal realised it still had thick cables running out the back. As the hand turned away the cables wrapped around its fingers, and no matter how much it tugged and twisted, it couldn't free itself. The wires ran deep into the junk pile, and the hand was stuck fast.

'We've got to cut it free,' said Hal.

'Shouldn't we leave it? There are more than enough boxes.'

'No, this is my fault and I'm going to fix it.'

— 15 —

One flew over the junk pile

Up close, the trapped hand was much bigger than
Hal expected. It had four fingers and a thumb, just
like humans, and it was trying to reach its own
wrist to pluck at the loops of cable. Hal felt in his
pocket for his trusty knife, then remembered his
parents had confiscated it. He'd whittled a short
plastic rod into a chess piece, only to discover the
innocent-looking thing was an expensive spare part
specially flown up from Gyris.

Hal looked around for something to cut the cords
with, then ducked as the second hand swept
overhead. It burrowed in the rubbish, and he
ducked again as it whizzed past with a broken
metal chair.

'I've got something,' shouted Alex.

Hal turned to see her holding up a slender piece
of metal. It was about a metre long, and one edge

was sharpened like a blade. A shadow swooped overhead, and Hal shouted a warning. Alex ducked, but the fingers darted in like lightning, plucking the strip of metal from her grasp. She cried out in pain and grabbed her hand. At first Hal was frozen in shock, but he recovered quickly, charging across the pile towards her. 'Are you all right?'

Fearfully, Alex held her hand out. They both looked at her tightly closed fingers, fearing the worst. Then, slowly, she uncurled them to reveal her palm. 'Phew, it's just a scratch,' said Alex.

Hal looked at the cut doubtfully. It looked quite deep to him. 'Are you sure?'

'I've had worse.'

'We'd better get it seen to. We'll go to the sickbay on level seven.'

'I said it's fine.' Alex pointed towards the mechanical hand, still struggling with the cables. 'Anyway, we've got to free Lefty.'

Hal was impressed. His friend Stinky would have yelled for a medic, and others he could name would have bawled for their mothers. 'All right, but keep your head down!'

They crossed the pile towards the trapped hand. On the way Hal picked up a piece of metal trim, which he hoped would cut the wires. The hand thrashed around as they got close, and junk slithered down the pile, crashing and bouncing on its way to the bottom. Hal glanced up to see a three-legged desk teetering near the top. It looked heavy, and if it came down on them it would do some real damage. 'Warn me if that desk slips. And watch the second hand closely.' He gripped the piece of trim and crawled closer, his mouth dry and his palms slick with sweat.

The hand appeared to be resting, and Hal saw several loops of cable around its big metal fingers. There was another round the wrist, and he decided to tackle that one first. He got closer and closer, brandishing the trim like a sword. Two metres . . . one metre . . .

Whoosh!

The hand balled into a fist and heaved with all its might, straining the cables. The junk pile shifted, throwing Hal off his feet, and he barely heard Alex's cry of alarm. Hal shielded his head with his arms and waited for the massive desk to come tumbling down.

Nothing happened, and Hal slowly uncovered his head. When he looked up he saw the desk was still there, hanging by a single bent leg. Nearby, the big hand had given up the struggle, and was lying on the junk pile with its palm up and its fingers curled.

Hal took a deep breath and talked to the hand. 'It's all right,' he said. 'I'm here to help.'

The fingers twitched.

Gripping his blade, Hal shuffled closer on all fours. He stretched the tip of the blade out until it touched the cable, then started to saw, trying to cut through the tough wires. Instead of cutting, the wires just moved back and forth in time with the blade. Hal got closer and grabbed the cable, then attacked it with the sharpened trim as though he were sawing planks.

Ping!

The cable parted, and Hal moved to the next. This one was tangled in and out of the big fingers, and he had to brace his knee on the huge palm and lean right across it. He hardly dared to breathe . . . if the hand closed now he'd be crushed like the old locker.

Poing!

The hand twitched as another cable parted. Three more to go, but he'd have to climb right over the palm to get to them. Then Hal heard movement right behind him, and he glanced round to see Alex holding out a longer piece of metal. This one had a serrated edge, and Hal took it thankfully. The longer blade made short work of the remaining cables, and then the hand was free.

Hal backed away quickly, expecting it to spring up and continue with its work. Instead, it just lay there. 'Do you think we killed it?'

'Of course not. It's just a machine.'

'Don't say that to a robot,' muttered Hal under his breath. He took up a metal pole and gave the hand a quick prod. Nothing. 'Maybe it doesn't realise it's free?'

'Maybe we should get out of here.'

'No, I have to get it going again.' Hal pushed the pole under the big fingers and tried levering them out of the pile. There was no reaction. Then he looked up at the desk, which was still balanced on top of the pile. What if he tipped that down so that it landed on the hand? That would wake it up!

He threw the pole aside and clambered up the mountain, his arms and legs burning from all the exercise. When he reached the top he tried freeing the desk, but it was stuck fast. He stood up, hoping to lever it free, and that's when Alex screamed a warning.

A shadow darted overhead, and before Hal knew what was happening the second hand grabbed him around the chest, pinning his arms. He was swept into the air and carried to the recycling machine, yelling and kicking his legs like mad. He landed on the conveyor belt with a thud, and it carried him straight towards the gaping mouth of the grinder. Even though he was facing certain death, a small part of his brain wondered what sort of goodies the huge machine would turn him into. Halburgers? Low-Hal yoghurt? Or maybe a big serve of Halghetti!

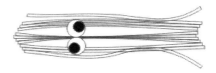

Hal flew towards the grinder on the fast-moving conveyor belt, still dazed by events. One second he'd been standing on top of the junk pile, the next he'd been swooping through the air. The thump of his landing had knocked the air from his lungs, but there was no time to stop and think. He sprang up and started running on the belt, going as fast as he could. His feet thudded on the rubber conveyor belt, and he felt like a jogger on the galaxy's biggest running machine. Out the corner of his eye he could see Alex slithering down the junk pile, leaping over obstacles as she hurried towards the big machine. Would she get help in time? Or would the hands scoop her up and add her to the menu?

Hal glanced over his shoulder. He was running at full speed, but the belt was too fast and he was still travelling backwards towards the grinder's gaping entrance. Inside he could see gears and wheels spinning and crashing together like huge mechanical teeth. He gulped and ran even faster.

One of the hands dropped a broken desk on the conveyor belt, right in front of him, and he leapt for all he was worth. He cleared it by millimetres, staggering as he landed back on the belt. Behind him the desk vanished inside the machine, and there were horrible crunching and cracking sounds as it was torn apart.

Hal was tiring now, and there were spots in front of his eyes. He was breathing fast but couldn't get enough air, and he desperately needed a rest. Just a few seconds!

Alex's face appeared over the side of the machine, and Hal's stomach sank. Why hadn't she gone for help?

'Can you jump out?' she called.

Hal shook his head. He had no breath to spare for talking.

'Okay. Wait there a minute.'

There was lots of things Hal could have said to that, but he contented himself with a roll of the eyes.

Thud!

An old storage tank landed on the belt, and Hal

forced his tired legs into a jump. His foot caught on the rounded surface but he staggered and regained his balance. The tank vanished into the machine with a squeal of tortured metal. He was much closer to the gaping maw now, and he could hear the *roar-roar-roar* of the spinning gears right behind him. His muscles burned like fire, and it was all he could do to keep running.

Then ... silence. The belt stopped dead but Hal kept going: straight off the far end of the belt, past the end of the machine, and halfway up the junk pile. He finally ran out of steam and collapsed on the ground. His chest heaved, his heart pounded and he felt rubbish pressing into the side of his face. Still, he was safe. Alex had done it!

Then came a voice, fierce and electronic and totally unexpected. 'Flibber my flash chips. What do you think you're doing!' .

Hal turned over, shielding his eyes against the overhead lights, and saw a tall bronze robot standing over him. Its eyes blazed a harsh red, and its thin face was arranged in a very angry expression. 'Tell me what you're doing here! Explain your presence immediately!'

16

Raging Reece

Hal opened and closed his mouth, unable to speak with the robot towering over him.

'This area is off limits to humans. Who sent you? Why are you spying on me?'

'I . . . we . . . ' stammered Hal, still shaken by his narrow escape.

Then Alex came hurrying up, and the robot spun round to confront her. 'Tangle my fibre optics!' it shouted, its eyes flashing like strobes. 'There's another one! Explain yourselves, right now!'

'W-we have a carty blank from Teacher,' managed Hal at last. Even to him, this sounded unconvincing. 'He told us to bring back some boxes.'

'Format my frontal lobes! Did you expect to find them inside the Recyclotron?'

'I didn't climb inside on purpose,' said Hal. 'One

of the hands got trapped, and when I freed it the other one grabbed me.'

'They could have turned you into mincemeat,' exclaimed the robot. 'Didn't you realise how dangerous they are?'

'I do now,' said Hal.

'You're not to go near this machine. Understood?'

Hal nodded.

'And these boxes . . . you thought you could sneak and take them?'

'No! I have a permission slip.'

'Show me.'

Hal dug in his pocket and took out the card, all crumpled and grubby. The robot frowned at it, then shepherded them towards the small office, watching closely in case they tried to steal his precious rubbish. When they got there he made them stand outside while he went in. Hal rubbed one corner of the dirty window with his sleeve, cleaning a small patch so he could peer into the robot's office.

The robot crossed to a battered old terminal, tapping its foot impatiently as it booted up. Hal's gaze travelled along the bench to a filing cabinet, across the old calendars on the wall, and down to a big recharging stand on the floor. He was about to look away when he saw flashing red and green lights over near the filing cabinet. He looked again, squinting hard, and frowned as he spotted a gleaming silver briefcase. It was heavy with a big lock on top, and it was identical to the one Alex's dad had been carrying. Hal nudged Alex and pointed, but before she could look the robot came back with the crumpled card.

'It seems this permission slip is in order, although I'm surprised they sent you all the way down here. Now tell me, how many boxes do you want to buy?'

'Buy?'

'Yes, or trade. Either works for me.'

'But ... Teacher needs them for class. You're supposed to give them to me.'

'He he hee!' The robot threw his head back and laughed. 'Ha ha ha! Give! That's a good one.'

'Why should we have to pay?' Hal frowned. 'We made them out of our own rubbish.'

'Listen to me, human. This area, this entire area, is mine.' The robot swept its arms around to illustrate its point. 'All the valuables, mine. All the treasure, mine.' It tapped its foot. 'This floor, mine.'

'Okay, okay. I get it.' Hal stood up. 'It's not treasure though. It's just piles of rubbish.'

The robot tapped the side of its nose, making a hollow donnnggg. 'That's why the concession was so cheap.'

'Con-what?'

'Bless my actuators, don't they teach you anything? A concession! Many years ago I bought the rights to this entire level. I'm entitled to everything I find here.'

'You paid money for all this rubbish?'

'Most certainly.'

'What do you do with it all?'

The robot was about to reply, then stopped. 'Your friend, is she all right?'

Hal glanced at Alex, who was staring through the office window. 'She's fine. Go on.'

'When supply ships visit the Space Station I sell them items made from recycled material.'

'Does the Commander know about this?'

'You bet your nobbly knee joints. The Space Station receives half my profit.'

'But Teacher works for the station, and he needs the boxes.'

'They're all mine,' said the robot stubbornly. 'If you want them you'll have to make me an offer.'

'You want me to pay for mouldy old boxes?'

'Boxes are made from cardboard, and cardboard comes from trees. There are no trees in space. You do the math.'

Alex glanced over her shoulder. 'Where I come from boxes are free.'

'Then I suggest you go back there and fetch some.' The robot turned back to Hal. 'Bring me something I can use and the boxes are yours.'

'You want more rubbish?'

'I prefer to call it raw material.'

'Okay, wait here. We'll be right back.' Hal grabbed Alex's elbow and turned for the exit. Then, for once, he remembered his manners. 'This is Alex and I'm Hal. What's your name?'

'I'm RC-KL-8, but humans call me Reece.'

17

Left Centre

'Did you see the briefcase on his desk?' murmured Hal, as they strode towards the exit. 'It looked exactly like your dad's.'

'It can't be,' said Alex firmly. 'I hid it in the cupboard.'

Hal remembered the flashing lights on the handle. 'Bet you it was his case.'

'I bet it wasn't.'

'Bet you five credits it was.'

'I bet you ten it wasn't.'

'Bet you fifty.'

'Bet you a hundred.'

'Done.'

Alex frowned. 'How will you pay?'

'I won't need to, because that was your dad's briefcase.'

'It wasn't!'

'I bet you two hundred.'

'Four!'

By the time the doors opened Hal was struggling to top Alex's latest bet. 'Nineteen planets, all the cash in the universe and two chocolate doughnuts,' he said at last. 'And no returns!'

They jogged along the corridors and stairways, using every one of Hal's special shortcuts to get back to the spares cupboard. When they got there Hal dragged the door open and peered into the darkness. 'Where did you put it?'

'That locker with the stickers on.'

With a horrible sense of foreboding, Hal opened the door wide. The light from the corridor flooded in and illuminated a hatch on the rear wall. The hatch had 'Warning' and 'Danger' and 'No Entry' signs all over it. 'Please tell me you didn't put it in there.'

'Sure! Who's going to ignore all those warnings?'

Silently, Hal activated the hatch. There was a whoosh as the doors parted, revealing a silver-lined hole. Alex clambered onto a cable drum and peered inside. 'There's a tunnel in here!' she said, her voice echoing as though she were standing at the top of a well. 'Where does it go?'

'All the way down to the recycling centre,' said Hal patiently. 'Face it, you chucked your dad's briefcase away.'

'How was I to know it was the recycling chute?' demanded Alex. She stepped off the drum with an angry look on her face. 'It's not fair! There's no sign!'

Hal checked behind the drum, where he found a plastic sign on the floor. He grabbed it and held it up: Warning! Recycling Chute! Danger! He checked the back and found a patch of dried glue. 'Someone didn't fix it properly, see? They must have used the wrong sort of glue.' Hal ran his hand over the wall. 'Yes, that's it. See, with this type of paint –'

'Never mind the stupid decor!' cried Alex. 'We've got to get that case back! My dad could ask for it any minute, and then I'd have to tell him I've lost it. He'll go completely mental!'

'Relax, will you? Let me think.'

'You said it would be safe in the cupboard. You promised!'

Then Hal had a thought. 'I know! We'll go and talk to my mum. She'll order Reece to give it back.'

'Oh yes, that's brilliant.   Let's march to A-section, talk our way past that bristle-haired guy at the security checkpoint, walk into the top secret meeting and tell everyone I lost my dad's briefcase.'

'All right, we'll find another adult. We'll explain, take them down to the recycling centre –'

'No!' Alex shook her head. 'You don't know my dad. If he finds out I lost his briefcase . . . '

'Why not blame me? I'm used to it.'

'You don't know my dad,' repeated Alex. 'I'm serious. We have to sort this out ourselves.'

Hal pondered for a moment, then snapped his fingers. 'I've got it. Back to the classroom.'

'You're not telling Teacher.'

'It's not Teacher I'm thinking about,' said Hal, as he ushered her out of the spares cupboard.

They'd barely set off for the classroom when Hal realised there was another problem. When they got back to class Teacher might take the permission slip away, and then they wouldn't be allowed back down to the recycling centre. Well . . . that was easily fixed. He took the card out and handed it to Alex.

'What's that for?'

'I'm going to class to organise something. In the meantime, see if you can find anything to swap for some boxes.'

'Are you mad?' protested Alex. 'Who cares about mouldy boxes? It's the briefcase we have to –'

'I know, I know. But we'll have to pretend we need boxes, or my plan won't work.'

'You have a plan?'

'Sure I do,' said Hal, hoping he sounded convincing. 'Now go and find some stuff to trade.'

'Where?'

That was the problem. Everything was scarce aboard a space station. Every sheet of paper, every scrap of food and every drop of water had to be flown in from the nearest planet, and that cost a lot of money. It was no wonder Reece hoarded everything that dropped through the chute. Hal racked his brains, but they couldn't just help themselves to stuff . . . theft was a serious crime. He wondered whether they should stake out a couple of recycling hatches, but they might wait around all day for someone to use them. Then Hal realised the answer to their problem. 'Why don't you go back to your dad's ship? There must be something you can take.'

'There might be,' said Alex doubtfully. 'What about you? Don't you have anything at home?'

'I'll have a look on the way back. Go on, hurry!'

Alex hesitated, but Hal's confidence was catching and she nodded briefly before running away at top speed. Hal was about to set off for the classroom when he heard her footsteps returning. 'What is it?'

'I don't know the way,' panted Alex.

'D nine, C twenty, B two. Can you remember that?'

'Got it.'

Alex charged off again, and Hal shouted advice after her. 'If you get lost, ask for help! And meet me at the lift afterwards!'

18

Secret Gang!

When Hal arrived at the classroom it was still busy. In fact, it was so busy Teacher was using three extra eyes, and they darted all over his electronic face as they tracked every movement. 'Stephen Binn, that is NOT how we handle chemicals. Please be careful. Melanie, put that roll of paper down immediately. No, I don't care which galaxy you're saving from evil invaders, it is NOT a death-dealing sword of doom. Braydon! Clean that up mess right now.'

Then Teacher spotted Hal. One eye studied his face while another pair checked his empty hands. 'No luck with the boxes, Hal Junior? Oh well. Return that permission slip and make yourself useful.'

'No, I can't. Someone's holding the boxes for me but I need to see Stinky first.'

'Very well, but you're not to distract him.' One of Teacher's eyes darted around to the side of his face, then stopped dead. 'In fact, I want you to tidy that bookcase first.'

Hal groaned. The bookcase was taller than he was and it had a dozen shelves crammed with books, equipment and craft projects. It would take ages! He turned back to Teacher, intending to plead for mercy, but the robot had already sped away. Resigned to the inevitable, Hal straightened a roll of plastic wrap and pulled a handful of books from the shelf. The screens lit up as he handled them, displaying vividly coloured scenes. He remembered some of them from his early school years, including one about a wandering dustbin robot and its shiny junk-collecting companion. He turned the pages, and was shocked to discover his one-time favourite was a morality tale about tidying your bedroom and helping your parents take the rubbish out. Disgusted, he straightened the books and crammed the foil on top. He eyed the remaining shelves, and was just wondering whether he could shift everything to someone else's bookcase when he had a brilliant idea. 'Hey, Natalie!'

A dark-haired girl spared him the briefest of glances. 'What do you want?'

'You like craft, don't you?'

'Hal Junior, if you think I'm tidying those shelves for you . . . '

'Nat, this is really important.'

Natalie eyed him shrewdly. 'What's it's worth?'

'I'll give you something valuable.'

'You're not fooling me again. Remember when I did your homework in exchange for a piece of wood from a real tree?'

'Sure.'

'It was plastic.'

'Just as well, because I got a C for that homework.' Hal thought for a moment. 'All right, tidy these shelves and you can join my secret gang.'

'What gang? I've never heard about any gang.'

'Of course you haven't. It wouldn't be secret if everyone knew about it.'

'Who else is in it?'

'Just Stinky and me. It's very exclusive.'

Natalie pursed her lips.

'Go on,' coaxed Hal. 'We have meetings and secret handshakes and everything.'

'All right, I'll do the shelves. But I want to be President!'

'Don't we all?' muttered Hal. He only hoped Natalie didn't quiz Stinky about the gang. First, because Stinky wasn't very good around girls, turning bright red and stammering when they looked at him. And second, because there wasn't any secret gang: Hal had only just invented it.

As he hurried across the classroom he decided a gang sounded like a fine idea. They could have a secret membership card, and meetings with lots of food, and they could even set up a roster where one member did everyone else's homework for the week. Hal decided to be leader, because then he could draw up the homework roster and make sure his name wasn't on it. Leaders also got the best food, the flashiest membership card and something called perks . . . at least, that's what he'd heard. Whenever his parents talked politics there was always mention of perks and parties, and if politicians could have them then Hal's gang would too. Then there was the recycling centre, with all those plastic wall panels. Maybe if he took Reece enough junk the robot would build them a clubhouse!

But first, the briefcase.

◆

'Stinky, do you have a minute?'

'I'm kind of busy,' said his friend, who was lining beakers up in the science cupboard.

'All right, I'll help you.'

Stinky looked doubtful. Hal plus glassware usually equalled destruction.

'I'll be extra careful. Promise!'

'All right. Hand me the beakers one by one.'

Hal dug into the box and came up with two of the graduated beakers. 'Hey Stinky?'

'Yep?'

'Catch!' Hal pretended to throw the beakers, and he grinned at Stinky's shocked expression.

'Stop messing about!' hissed Stinky.

'All right, all right.' Hal passed a beaker over, then glanced around to make sure nobody was listening. When he was sure he wouldn't be overheard, he lowered his voice and explained quickly about the briefcase in the recycling centre.

'Why don't you tell Teacher?'

'Alex won't let me.'

Stinky's brow creased as he tackled the problem, and Hal could almost hear his friend's brain whirring. If anyone could find the solution, it was Stinky!

Finally, he spoke. 'You have to think of it like a chess problem. It's a classic feint situation.'

'How's fainting going to help?' demanding Hal. 'You think if we collapse in a heap this robot will take pity on us?'

'Feint, not faint. It's an e, not an a.'

Hal grumbled under his breath. He'd come to Stinky for help, not a spelling lesson.

'A feint is when you distract your opponent with one hand, then use the other to achieve your goal.'

Hal brightened. 'The recycling machine had hands. Are you saying we should stuff Reece into it?' Then he frowned. 'Won't someone notice he's missing?'

'I was referring to hands in a metaphorical sense.'

Hal blinked. 'Meta whatter?'

'They were just an example. A feint could involve hands, armies –'

'Sleevies?' suggested Hal.

Stinky struggled to keep a straight face. 'I meant troops, Hal.'

'Where are we supposed to get a bunch of warriors

from?' demanded Hal indignantly. 'I came to you for ideas, not impossible suggestions.'

'Look, let's start again.'

'No, let's not. Alex and I will march down there, demand the case back and . . . and . . . ' Hal's voice tailed off. Demanding anything from Reece was almost as crazy as Stinky's fainting invasion force.

'Hal, the answer is simple. One of you goes back for the boxes, and while Reece is busy the other one snatches the case. Is that clear?'

'Now that's more like it. Much better than your feint idea.'

'Er, y-yes.'

'Two problems. One, he won't give us the boxes.'

'Right. You'll need something to trade.'

Hal eyed the beakers. 'What about these?'

'No! You can't trade away vital equipment!'

Hal would have traded all of the classroom equipment for a jam doughnut, but Stinky wouldn't be swayed. 'What do you suggest?'

'Perhaps something of your own. Do you have any old toys you don't play with?'

Hal saw Natalie grinning to herself, and he reddened. 'I do not play with toys!'

'There you go then. You can give them all to Reece. What was the other problem?'

'I can't sneak into his office without getting caught.'

'You need a distraction.' Stinky rubbed his chin, and Hal knew his friend's brain was busy on the problem.

While Stinky was thinking, Hal looked around the classroom for inspiration. He spotted the recycling hatch with its red and yellow warning signs, and a frown crossed his face. That hatch led to the chute, and the chute led to the recycling centre.

Hal's gaze travelled from the hatch, to the cardboard box at his feet, and back to the hatch. A plan was slowly forming, but he was going to need help. 'Stinky, do you have any matches?'

'What?'

Hal pushed the cardboard box with his toe. 'You could light this thing and toss it down the hatch.'

'Haven't you learnt your lesson?' Stinky was scandalised. 'You can't go around lighting more fires! Don't you know how dangerous –'

'All right, calm down.' Hal eyed the chemicals on the shelf. 'Do you remember that experiment I did? The one with my patented green smoke?'

'Vividly.'

'Reckon you could mix a batch?'

'What, here?'

'Yes here.' Hal nodded towards the recycling

chute. 'Make up a smoke bomb and chuck it down there. While Reece's busy climbing the junk pile to investigate, I'll nab the briefcase.'

'I could get in awful trouble.'

'Tell 'em it was me.'

'No, Hal. I won't do it. Throwing smoke bombs is seriously bad news. I could get detention, or I could get a . . . a . . . ' Stinky swallowed. 'Hal, I could get a B from Teacher!'

'I'm not talking about a real bomb, it's just a few harmless chemicals. It'll clear in a minute or two, right?'

'Maybe five,' said Stinky, wavering a little.

Hal looked at his watch. 'Give me twenty minutes, then drop the smoke bomb. Got it?'

'What if it's not ready?'

Hal felt a rush of relief. His friend was going to help! 'Of course it'll be ready.'

'What if Teacher asks where you've gone?'

'I've gone to fetch his boxes. And that's the truth.' At that moment Hal saw Natalie making a beeline for them. He grabbed Stinky and quickly demonstrated a secret handshake.

'What's that for?' asked Stinky.

'Trust me, you're going to need it.'

19

MINT! R@RE!

Hal left the classroom and set off for E-section, jogging at top speed. With all this running around he was beginning to wish for a jet-powered scooter. He wondered whether his parents would get him one for his birthday, but unfortunately they were more likely to get him some exciting new homework software. Parents were odd like that.

On his way home he kept an eye out for handy piles of rubbish, discarded trash and unwanted junk. Unfortunately the corridors were as spotless as ever. When he reached his cabin he opened the doors under his bunk and peered inside. There was a planet rover with a broken wheel, the paint battered and peeling. He delved deeper and came up with a broken toy wand, a crumpled wizard hat and a stuffed owl left over from some fancy dress outfit. The owl was missing one tufty ear and both of its eyes, and so much stuffing had leaked out it was as flat as a pancake. Hal dug around some more, but there was nothing else he was prepared to part with. The big orange ray gun still made a decent 'Brrrr' sound when he pulled the trigger, and he didn't want to give up the battered old 20-sided dice . . . not until he found out which game it belonged to. There was also an old book about tiny people living under floorboards - whatever those were - but that belonged to Hal's dad and he knew it would be missed.

Gathering up his spoils, Hal could only hope that Alex had found something more useful. He threw the toys into a bag and hurried towards the lift.

◆

Hal met Alex near the lift in D-section, and he could tell right away that she hadn't had much luck. Her expression was downcast and she was hiding something behind her back.

'Go on then,' said Hal, trying to sound encouraging. 'What did you get?'

Reluctantly, Alex opened her hand to reveal . . . a blue button from a jumper and a muscled forearm from an action figure. 'These are all I could find.'

'Are you kidding? They're not going to buy us anything!'

'So what did you get?'

Hal showed her the truck and the pieces of fancy dress.

'What's Reece going to do with a weedy old stick?' demanded Alex. 'And the glove puppet . . . what's that all about?'

'It's a stuffed owl,' said Hal defensively.

'You're not wrong. Still, it's better than the grotty old hat.'

'You can talk!' said Hal hotly. 'All you found was an arm and a lousy button!'

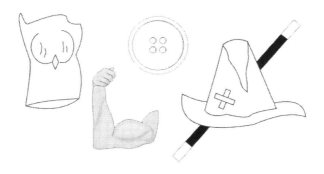

They eyed their haul in silence, uncertain of their next move. Should they hunt around for more junk, or take what they had back to Reece and haggle. 'I vote we go back to your dad's ship,' said Hal. 'I bet I'll find something if I go through his stuff.'

'You can't!' said Alex in alarm, as she pictured Hal carting off armloads of valuables. 'My dad would kill me!'

'I guess you're right,' said Hal reluctantly. 'Okay, we'll see what Reece will give us for this lot. You can keep that button though - we don't want to insult him.'

When they reached the recycling centre Reece was sorting a pile of old fabric. Hal wondered whether he unpicked them all and knitted new clothes from the thread, or just sold them as bundles of cleaning rags.

'Burnish my bronze heels!' exclaimed the robot, when he spotted Hal and Alex. 'What do you have for me?'

Somewhat embarrassed, Hal displayed the motley collection of toys.

'Interesting.' Reece picked over the items. 'I can give you half a dozen boxes for these.'

'Done,' said Hal quickly, before the robot could change its mind. 'Can we help ourselves?'

'And have you sneak a couple of extras? No way!' Reece tapped himself in the chest. Clonggg! 'I'll pick them out for you.'

They crossed to a big pile of folded boxes, where the robot started picking out matching sizes. While he was busy there was a clatter from the middle of the recycling centre. Hal glanced round, hoping to see a cloud of smoke, but instead a stream of junk poured through the roof to land on the big pile. He eyed his watch and realised Stinky wouldn't be ready yet. He had to slow Reece down, or the whole plan would fail.

Unfortunately Reece wasn't waiting around for Stinky, or Hal, or anyone else's special plans. Within seconds he'd gathered six neatly folded boxes. 'There you are. All present and correct.'

'Sorry, they're no good.'

'Fan my fibre optics!' said Reece sharply. 'Why ever not? What's wrong with them?'

'They've got writing on. Teacher wants plain ones.'

'What are you talking about?' demanded Alex. 'Who cares whether –'

Hal nudged her. 'Look, there's a plain one at the bottom of the pile. I'm sure it won't take long to find five more.'

Reece turned to look at them, his arms full of boxes. 'Did you say these are no good?'

'I'm afraid not,' said Hal. 'We need plain ones. It's for a . . . craft project. Right Alex?'

'Er . . . sure. Writing would spoil it.'

Reece looked at the pile. 'It'll take some time to find six plain boxes. They're not very common.'

'Good.' Hal hesitated. 'I mean, it's good of you to help us.'

'They're probably worth more than the printed ones,' said Reece, a cunning look in his eye. 'Do you have any more valuables?'

'No. I mean, yes. We bought a very special item.' Hal held his hand out to Alex. 'Pass me the firing mechanism from that space gun.'

Alex looked blank. 'The which from the what?'

'That blue circular device with mounting holes.'

'You mean the bu–'

'No, I mean the firing mechanism.' Hal clicked his fingers impatiently. 'Come on, I know it's incredibly rare and valuable but we need those boxes. You'll just have to give it up.'

Reece was almost licking his lips by now, and when Alex took out the blue button and dropped it on Hal's palm the robot's eyes were the size of dinner plates. 'By the patenting of my source code. Is that really a firing mechanism?'

Hal was about to say yes, but he couldn't bring himself to lie. 'I saw one just like this in a book,' he said, neglecting to mention it was a sewing book.

'Would you take ten boxes for it?'

'Twenty.'

'I don't have twenty.'

'All right, ten boxes plus one extra item of my choice.'

Reece looked uncertain. 'I'm not sure about that. You might choose something far more valuable than a firing mechanism.'

Privately, Hal thought every scrap of junk in the recycling centre was more valuable than a single blue button, but he wasn't about to say so. 'Ten boxes plus one item of my choice. Yes or no?'

'Done.'

'Let's shake on it.' Hal spat on his hand and held it out to the robot, who eyed it doubtfully. 'Go on. This is as good as a contract.'

Reece still looked uncertain, and in the end he shook hands so quickly Hal barely felt it.

'Right. One firing mechanism coming up.' Hal gave Reece the button, and after a quick inspection the robot opened a small door in its chest and placed the treasured item inside. Then ... *whizz, zip, slither, grab!* Reece sorted the boxes in no time.

'Ten plain ones,' said the robot proudly.

'No, no, no!' Hal put on his best Teacher impersonation, rolling his eyes and shuffling backwards and forwards on the spot as though his feet had turned into wheels. 'This won't do. This won't do at all!'

'What is it?' asked a harassed-looking Reece. 'What's wrong this time?'

'These boxes are grey! I said brown. Brown!'

'You said no such thing!' protested Reece angrily.

'I did so!' Hal turned to Alex, who was trying not to laugh. 'Did I say grey?'

'No, you definitely didn't say grey.'

'Told you so!' Hal dug up another of Teacher's favourite lines. 'Do it properly, or don't do it at all.'

'Humans!' muttered Reece, turning back to the pile. He picked through the boxes with sharp, angry movements, keeping up a running commentary under his breath. 'Brown ones ... plain ones ... writing ... no writing. Rattle my receptors! Why can't they make up their minds?'

Meanwhile, Hal still needed an excuse to get near the office. 'Reece, can I get a drink of water?'

'Rust my radio receptors!' Reece shuddered. 'There's no water down here. Horrible nasty stuff!' He turned to the pile of boxes and sorted through them, muttering under his breath about the dangers of h's and o's.

It wasn't quite what Hal had planned, but at least Reece's back was turned. While the robot was

distracted Hal slipped away, making for the office.
The briefcase would soon be his!

— 20 —

Ten Star Hotel

There was just one problem. How was Hal going to enter the office without being seen? He needed a disguise, of course! He eyed a bundle of material with garish flowers all over it, and shuddered. If anyone expected him to disguise himself as a sofa they had another think coming.

Then he spotted a big packing crate, nearly as tall as he was. It was just like the ones in the arcade game, but was it hollow? He hurried over to tap on it, and smiled when he heard the echoes. The crate was made from plastic, and it had a big square lid. Perfect!

Seconds later he'd discarded the lid and tipped the crate right over. He found a sharp piece of metal and bored a peephole through the side, then raised the bottom and slipped underneath. It was pitch black inside, with the only light coming through his makeshift eye-hole. He made another hole to his left, the side facing Reece and Alex, then threw the piece of metal aside and stood up. He bent his neck and took the weight of the packing crate on his shoulders, staggering forwards a few steps before setting it down. Then he peered through the hole. The others were busy with the boxes, and hadn't noticed him. It was working!

Hal made his way towards the office, step by step. Now and then the crate bumped into a rubbish pile or jammed on a piece of junk, and each time this happened he had to dart from one eyehole to the other - first to see if Reece was watching, and then to see if he was about to run into anything.

Before long he was right outside the office door, and he allowed himself a triumphant smile. Who said computer games never taught you anything?

◆

Hal peered out of the crate and watched Reece and Alex sorting boxes. First Reece would scrabble through the pile until he found something, and then Alex would consider it from every angle before shaking her head. The robot was getting more annoyed by the minute, and Hal hoped Alex didn't overdo it.

Hal also kept an eye on the recycling chute, because any minute now Stinky's distraction would arrive to shatter the peace. Hal looked at his watch. Any second now, in fact.

Time passed, and Hal glared at his watch, muttering under his breath. Had Stinky forgotten the plan? Or had Teacher spotted him mixing chemicals, and marched him straight off to the Station Commander? Either way, Stinky had let him down.

Hal realised he needed a new plan. What if he sneaked into the office, took the briefcase and made his way to the far end of the recycling centre? Once there he could make a big show of 'discovering' the briefcase under a pile of junk. Hopefully Reece wouldn't realise it was the briefcase from his office, and would let Hal take the 'new' one in exchange for the so-called firing pin.

Hal didn't think it was a particularly good plan, so he tried again. This involved grabbing the briefcase and running for the exit as fast as he could. As long as he got there first, he'd be able to close the doors and escape. Otherwise . . . Hal shook his head. He didn't want to think what might happen if Reece caught him. Then he spotted a pretty big flaw in this new plan: Reece might not catch him, but the unpleasant robot would certainly catch Alex.

That was it, then. He'd just have to use plan A.

At that moment there was a rattle-bang from the recycling chute, followed by a loud FFFFFsshhh! Hal stared out of the crate and saw thick green smoke billowing from the top of the biggest junk pile. The evil-looking smoke rolled down the side of the pile, and from a distance it looked like an erupting volcano. Stinky had done it!

Reece took one look at the smoke and charged away from Alex like a bronze streak. The robot ran incredibly fast, his legs a blur as he bounded over piles of junk. When he reached the big pile he ran straight up the side without slowing, heading for the smoky summit.

After seeing how quickly the robot could move, Hal realised he only had seconds to grab the briefcase and escape. He lifted the edge of the crate and squeezed out, then ran into the office. Behind him he could hear junk slithering down the pile as Reece hunted for the source of the smoke. As soon as those noises stopped, the robot would be back again.

Hal took three steps towards the filing cabinet, ready to grab the briefcase, then stopped dead. It wasn't there! He spun round and saw it immediately - it was sitting on the desk, and it was wide open! The case was empty but there was a thick file sitting alongside, and Hal guessed Reece had taken it out. He glanced at the cover, which was an artist's impression of a space station with 'Hotel Grande Luxe' picked out in shiny gold lettering. The station looked like the Oberon, but he guessed they made them all from similar plans.

A wisp of green smoke drifted in through the door, and Hal realised Stinky's concoction was working better than expected. He peered through the grimy window and saw a sea of green fog with junk piles poking out like islands in a lagoon. Reece was stamping on something with both feet, while green smoke continued to pour down the slope like a slow-moving river. Nearby Hal could see Alex standing with her back to the office, her head and shoulders just above the green fog.

Hal picked up the file and flipped through the

glossy pages, which were full of headings like 'Income projection' and 'Handover strategy'. Typical adults, using a cool electronic briefcase to store a boring report.

Hal shrugged, and he was about to throw the file back in the briefcase when Alex came barging into the office. 'He's coming!' she breathed. 'Hide . . . quick!'

21

Getting Deskerate

Hal looked around the pokey little office. They could hardly cram themselves into the filing cabinet's drawers, and Reece's charger stand wouldn't have hidden a ham sandwich, let alone two children. That only left the big desk.

Hal dropped to his hands and knees and scuttled into the darkness. Alex followed, and the two of them sat side by side with their backs to the wall. They wrapped their arms around their knees to draw their feet in, away from the pool of light shining on the office floor.

Then Hal remembered something, and his heart sank. He was still holding the report! Was there time to put it back on the desk? No, a shadow fell across the floor as Reece came in, and Hal sank back into the shadows. Did the robot have heat sensors? A super sense of smell? Laser-guided eyes? More importantly, would he notice the report was missing?

There was a creak as Reece sat down and a squeak as he pushed his pointed metal feet under the desk, narrowly missing Hal's shins. The robot was clearly annoyed, tutting and muttering under his breath.

'Crumble my circuit boards! First they want boxes, then they want plain boxes, then they want brown boxes and now they want no boxes. Small humans are worse than the big ones!'

There was a lot more of this in a similar vein, and Hal soon realised their predicament. Robots didn't have tea breaks or lunch breaks, and they certainly didn't have toilet breaks. In fact, Reece probably worked 24 hours a day, seven days a week. So how long were they going to be stuck under the desk, waiting for a chance to leave?

Hal spent the time dreaming up escape plans. His first idea was to jump up, shout 'boo' and then run like fury while the robot recovered its senses. Problem was, robots didn't have senses to recover from, and their reactions were so fast Reece would have Hal in a headlock before he could say 'b' . . . let alone the 'oo!' part.

Hal's next idea was to communicate with Stinky and ask for more help. Unfortunately he was stuck under a desk and there were no handy water pipes to tap morse code on. Anyway, the second he tried to bash out a message, Reece would look under the desk to see where the tap-tap-tappity-tap was coming from.

So, it all came down to Hal's final option: to distract the robot. Could he send it away somehow? He'd seen a show on ventriloquism once, where a performer threw his voice and made it sound like his dummy was speaking. What if Hal threw his voice to the terminal and made out there was a fire alarm? Trouble was, whenever he tried to throw his voice it always sounded like he was gargling through his nose.

Hal's elbow was getting sore where it was pressed against the hard floor, and any minute now his stomach was going to start rumbling. He had to do something!

Another ten minutes dragged past, and by now Hal was ready to give himself up. He put one hand down and started to move, but at that moment Reece pushed the chair back and stood up. Hal heard the robot moving around, and there was a loud *click!* Hal frowned as he tried to remember the layout of the office, and his spirits soared when he remembered what was on that particular wall. What was the one thing robots had to do? Recharge themselves!

Very slowly, Hal moved his head until he could see the robot's chest, then its neck, then its jaw . . . He tried to lean forward some more, to see whether Reece's eyes were open, but Alex pulled him back. He frowned at her but she just scowled, gesturing at the charger then shaking her head firmly. Her meaning was clear: don't risk getting seen!

That was all very well, but how long were they supposed to sit there? Did robots switch off when they charged up, or would Reece spot them the minute they tried to escape?

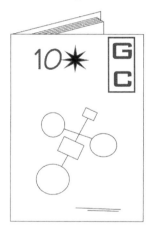

Sitting still was torture at the best of times, but the floor was rock hard under the desk, and every time Hal tried to get comfortable Alex would scowl at him and put her finger to her lips. To make things worse, she was able to sit like a statue.

In the end Hal decided to skim the report, hoping to find something - anything - to pass the time. After two or three pages he saw a section titled 'Resettlement Options', and vague memories of settlers and exploration had him reading in no time. Unfortunately, instead of gripping tales of survival and daring, the report contained a load of dry sentences with enormously long words.

Hal skimmed it all twice, but it didn't make a whole lot of sense. It went on and on about hiring and firing, retraining scientists and 'the benefits of multi-skilling' . . . whatever that meant. Then two words leapt out at him:

Gyris and Oberon!

Hal looked at the text again. Sure enough, the local planet got a mention, and right underneath he saw a sentence that made his blood run cold:

As soon as the scientists have been removed from Space Station Oberon, construction will start on the first hotel rooms.

Hal closed the report and stared at the space station on the cover. It didn't just LOOK like the Oberon. It WAS the Oberon! Grogan was going to take over Hal's home and turn it into a hotel!

22

Infilcrate

Hal felt Alex tugging his sleeve. He was still staring at the report in shock, but eventually she got his attention. When he turned to look he realised she was pointing to her flashy space watch. Hal frowned back. His home was at stake and she wanted to watch a movie?

Then Alex held the watch under his nose, and Hal realised there was a curt message on the screen:

Take briefcase to security checkpoint ASAP.

Hal groaned. Could things get any worse? They were trapped in Reece's office, the briefcase lock had been picked and the contents were gripped in Hal's fingers. Now they had to put the report back, seal the briefcase, sneak past Reece and return everything . . . all before they were discovered!

Hal eyed the report, and then he noticed something tucked inside the back page. It was a sheet of thick paper, folded in two, and when he opened it out he saw fancy writing across the top: Letter of Agreement. There was an important-looking seal in one corner, a mass of small print in the middle, and then a dozen different signatures at the bottom. He glanced at Alex but she was busy tapping a reply on her watch.

'I'm telling him we're on the way,' she whispered. 'That should buy us some time.'

On the spur of the moment, Hal folded the letter and crammed it into his pocket.

Alex finished sending her reply, then shot Hal a worried look. 'Now what?'

'I don't k—'

Before he could finish the sentence there was a commotion from the recycling centre:

Rattle-clatter-thud!

FFFFFsshhh! FFFFFsshhh! FFFFFSSHHH!

Hal frowned. What was that?

Chack!

Reece was out of the charger like a shot, his feet pounding on the floor as he ran out of the office. Hal and Alex tumbled out from under the desk, groaning as circulation returned to their cramped legs. Hal got up gingerly and hobbled to the window, where he saw something that made his spirits soar. It wasn't just a green smoke bomb filling the centre

. . . no, there were half a dozen! Purple smoke, blue smoke, orange smoke . . . there was even a vibrant shade of pink that made Hal wince.

The result was like an explosion in a paint factory, with a riot of colours flowing around the piles of junk. Reece was almost invisible in the multi-coloured smoke, although Hal could just see him jumping up and down and shaking his metal fists at the recycling shaft. Hal grinned at the sight. Good old Stinky! He must have figured out they were trapped, and the new smoke bombs were exactly what they needed to escape.

Hal didn't waste any time. He threw the report into the briefcase and jammed the lid shut. The indicator lights blinked and there was a *click!* as the lock armed itself. 'Come on. Run!'

Reece had already smothered two of Stinky's smoke bombs, and the rest wouldn't last long. Was there enough time to run for the exit? No. Hal looked around for inspiration and spotted the large crate he'd used earlier. He grabbed Alex by the arm and together they lifted one edge of the crate and scrambled inside.

'On my count,' he said. 'Ready? One, two . . . go!'

They both straightened, lifting the base off the ground, and shuffled forward with the weight on their shoulders. Hal tried to match Alex's strides, but it was impossible to tell if they were going in a straight line. After a while he had to let his end down, and they stopped for a breather. Hal put his eye to the hole but all he could see was thick swirling smoke.

They lifted the packing crate and started moving again.

Thump!

The crate stopped dead and they both fell over. Hal got up and peered through the hole, where he saw the vague outline of a junk pile directly ahead. 'Turn right,' he whispered.

'Shouldn't that be left?'

'We'll go left next.'

They made their way around the pile, the big crate swaying and bumping, until Hal judged they were on the other side. Then they set off again, moving as fast as they dared.

They hit five more junk piles on their way to the exit, turning this way and that until Hal barely knew up from down, let alone left from right. Then he saw a big grey wall and realised they must have made it. There was no breath for talking, so he gestured at Alex and together they heaved the crate over.

Crash! It tipped on its side and they were free at last. Hal ran to the wall and followed it to the right, looking for the exit. It seemed a long way, and then he stopped, puzzled, as they came to a corner. He shrugged and turned right again, following the wall. Even if they went all the way round, they'd find the exit sooner or later.

Thud!

Hal frowned. The noise was directly ahead, and it sounded familiar.

Thud!

Then he realised what it was. They were nowhere near the exit ... they'd gone all the way around the edge and ended up near the huge recycling machine. And Reece was between them and the exit!

'I told you we were going the wrong way!' protested Alex.

'No, it was the right way. You turned the crate too much.'

'*I* turned it? You kept walking into things!'

'Not half as many as you did. You weren't going fast enough.'

Alex displayed the briefcase. 'Holding this? I'd like to see you try.'

They were crouching behind an old filing cabinet, and Hal risked a quick look towards the office. The smoke was clearing now, and he could see Reece slithering down the big pile of junk. How long before the robot realised the briefcase was missing?

'We'd better get back into the crate,' said Alex.

'No, we'll stay put. He might go back in the charger.'

Alex tapped her watch. 'We can't stop. Dad's waiting for me.'

Squeak, squeak, squeak.

Hal frowned. They didn't have mice aboard the space station, more's the pity, so what was making that noise?

Squeak, squeak .... squeak.

Whatever it was, it had stopped just the other side of the filing cabinet. Hal raised his head for a look ... and came face to face with a powered trolley. For a split second he thought it was Carrie, come to rescue them, but then he noticed the battered paintwork and the bent rear wheel. It was Paul, Carrie's missing friend!

Meanwhile, Paul had also noticed Hal, and the trolley was backing away slowly. 'D-don't recycle me,' he said in a quavering voice. 'I'll work harder, I promise!'

'It's all right,' hissed Hal. 'We're friends! Carrie sent us to find you!'

'Y-you know Carrie?' asked the trolley, and this time there was a note of hope in his voice.

'Absolutely.' Hal beckoned. 'Come round this side where Reece can't see you.'

'Reece is watching me?' The trolley went back and forth on the spot, its buckled wheel dragging on the ground. 'Oh no, not Reece. Reece doesn't like me. Like me! Tee hee hee!'

Hal realised Paul was near breaking point, and after a quick look towards the office he vaulted over the filing cabinet and hurried to the trolley. He crouched next to it, put one hand on the battered metal surface and spoke in a low, calm voice. 'Listen to me, okay? Whatever happened to you before, it's over. I'm here now, and nobody hurts my friends. Do you understand?'

'B-but Reece . . . '

'If that tin can comes near you I'll feed him into the Recyclotron,' said Hal fiercely.

This did the trick, and Paul calmed down. 'Will I be working in the kitchens again? I like the kitchens.'

'If you help me you can work wherever you like.' Hal glanced towards the office, but there was no sign of Reece. 'Do you ever leave the recycling centre?'

'Sometimes I take deliveries to the lift.'

'Perfect. Can you do one now?'

'I-I suppose so.'

'Follow me.' Hal led the trolley back around the filing cabinet, where Alex was waiting impatiently. First he explained about Paul, and then he outlined his plan. 'But first we're going to need a few things . . . '

23

Paul the other one

Squeak, squeak, squeak.

Reece looked up from his terminal, a frown creasing his metal forehead. What was that confounded trolley doing now? It was supposed to be ferrying raw materials to the Recyclotron, not going on joyrides! Reece pushed his chair back and strode to the door. What he saw outside had him blinking with amazement. 'What the –'

'The delivery is ready, sir.'

Paul was draped with a tatty tablecloth, and his upper shelf was covered with an assortment of plates, cups and cutlery.

'Buff my ball joints,' said Reece. 'Who ordered that mess?'

'It's an urgent delivery for the kitchen. There's a VIP on board the Space Station and they've run out of cutlery.'

'Is that so?' Reece felt a surge of joy. 'Running out' meant a shortage, and a shortage meant a fat profit. 'What am I getting in return?'

Paul hesitated, almost as though he were listening to instructions. 'You can have all the refuse from the visitor's ship.'

'Foreign muck!' Reece rubbed his hands together. 'Excellent! You may proceed!'

'As you wish, sir.'

Squeak-squeak-squeak went the trolley, and Reece eyed it in surprise. He'd never seen it move that fast before! Then he forgot about Paul and returned to his desk, where he sat down to bask in his good fortune. What with the rare space gun firing mechanism, the exceptionally fine briefcase and now this unexpected bonus shipment, it had been a rubbishy day to remember. That's when he looked down at his empty desk, and the truth hit him like a sledgehammer.

The briefcase . . . someone had stolen it!

❧

Squeaksqueaksqueaksqueak!

'You've got to slow down!' cried Alex, as the trolley rocketed along the corridor.

144

'No!' shouted Hal. 'Faster, faster!'

Alex grabbed his arm. 'It's going to look pretty suspicious if he breaks the sound barrier.'

Hal was enjoying the wild ride, but he realised she was right. The tatty tablecloth was tearing itself to shreds, and they'd lost several cups and plates at the last corner.

Screeeeech!

Paul took another corner at speed, and this time he nearly lost Alex.

'All right, Paul. Slow it down a bit.'

'Got . . . to . . . escape,' puffed the trolley. 'Got . . . to . . .'

'You can still escape, but slower.'

'Under . . . stood.'

Their pace slowed, and moments later they rolled into the elevator.

'Where to?' demanded Alex, who was closest to the buttons.

'Level nineteen.'

Alex was still reaching out when they heard footsteps pounding along the corridor.

'It's Reece!' hissed Hal. 'He must have discovered the missing case!'

Alex pressed the button and the doors started to close. Paul backed away, trying to avoid being spotted through the closing gap, and Hal only just shifted his fingers before the trolley ground against the wall. The footsteps got closer and closer, and they could hear Reece muttering to himself.

'Thieves! Robbers! Jumble my joints, I'll make them pay for this!'

Thud! The doors met in the middle just as Reece jabbed his finger on the call button with an impatient click-click-click! Hal held his breath, hoping the doors wouldn't open again, then sighed in relief as the lift shot upwards. They weren't clear yet, though . . . the robot would be straight after them.

On the other hand . . . Hal smiled as a plan came to him, and he pressed the button for level seven.

When the doors opened there was a delicious smell of baking, and Hal nodded towards the right-hand passage.

'The kitchens?' said Alex. 'What are we doing here?'

Hal just smiled and patted the trolley. 'Come on, Paul. You're nearly home!'

Paul drove out of the lift and started up the corridor. He was going a lot more slowly now, and Hal realised the high-speed run had drained the batteries. He looked back along the corridor and saw the lift doors closing. Hopefully Reece would take the bait and head straight for level nineteen.

Paul drove them all the way to the canteen, despite getting slower and slower. His batteries were almost gone but he pushed on regardless, focusing on getting home. They reached the last pair of doors, where Hal called a halt. 'Wait here, the pair of you.' He got out and opened the doors, slipping through the gap into the kitchen. A minute later he was back, carrying a folded tablecloth under his arm. He shook it out and draped it over Paul.

'That's not going to help much,' said Alex. 'He needs batteries, not a new skirt.'

'It's just a disguise.'

There was a sudden burst of music, making them both jump. The noise came from Alex's watch, and the screen was pulsing in a range of colours. 'It's my dad,' she said urgently. 'He's calling me!'

'Hang up on him,' said Hal.

Alex hesitated, then gave her arm a shake. 'Yes dad?'

'Where are you? I've been waiting fifteen minutes!'

Hal was standing two metres away, but he could still hear Grogan's angry voice.

'I, er, got lost. We're almost there.'

'That's not acceptable, Alex. You've let me down.'

'I'm sorry, dad. We'll be quick, I promise.'

'You need to learn the value of time. When you get to the checkpoint I want you to stand there for thirty minutes before you call me. And make sure you're holding my briefcase the whole time!'

There was a burst of static as Grogan cut the connection, and Alex lowered the watch. 'Thirty minutes! My arms will fall off.'

'Don't worry,' said Hal stoutly. 'I'll hold the briefcase for you.'

'Thanks, but he'd find out,' muttered Alex. 'And what about Reece? If we stand around that checkpoint for half an hour he'll spot us for sure, and then he'll take the briefcase back.'

'We'll explain to the guard. He'll protect the briefcase.' Privately Hal doubted Stinky's brother Richard would stand up to Reece, but they'd worry about that when it happened. 'Come on, we've got to organise a lift.' Hal opened the doors, and Alex helped him wheel Paul into the kitchen. On the far side several chefs were busy preparing another course, while helpers scraped plates and washed

148

up. Nearby there was another trolley with an identical tablecloth . . . Carrie!

Hal guided Paul to the wall, then crouched next to Carrie. 'It's us again,' whispered Hal. 'Can you hear me?'

'Loud and clear,' murmured the trolley.

'Don't make a fuss, but we've rescued Paul.'

'For real?'

'Yes, he's right behind you. We're going to plug him in for a charge, and then I need your help.'

'Anything!' whispered Carrie.

'We need a lift to A-section.'

'Easy. Hop aboard.'

Moments later they were ready. Carrie drove for the door, and Hal could just see Alex's worried expression in the darkness. He gave her a confident smile. 'Don't worry, it'll be okay!' Secretly, he wondered how everything was going to turn out. The agreement he'd taken from the briefcase was folded in his pocket, and if Grogan was mad now, what was he going to be like when he discovered it was missing? Hal had no intention of putting it back, not if he could prevent the Space Station being turned into a luxury hotel.

24

A-Section

Carrie rolled along the corridor towards the lift, the ride smooth and effortless compared to Paul with his buckled, squeaky wheel. They were only halfway there when they heard pounding footsteps in the distance. Carrie turned sharp left, and Hal heard the hiss of a closing door. He peered out and realised they were hiding in someone's private cabin. Fortunately the owner wasn't there.

A second later they heard Reece's angry muttering as he charged past. 'Energise my electrics! I'll teach you, you sneaky little thieves. Steal from me would you?'

The footsteps receded, and Hal was just relaxing again when Carrie spoke. 'Was that a friend of yours?'

'Er, not exactly.'

'Good. Reece's a rather unpleasant character.'

There was a hiss as the door opened, and Carrie raced along the corridor before stopping at the lift. 'You know Reece works in the recycling centre?'

'Someone did mention it,' said Hal casually.

'Just let me know if he bothers you. I have a score to settle with that –'

Ting!

'The lift's here. Floor please?'

Hal lifted the tablecloth and pressed the button for level nineteen. It was time to deliver the briefcase.

'We really appreciate this,' said Alex, as the lift carried them towards the higher levels. 'Are you sure you won't get into trouble?'

'Probably, but what can they do?' Carrie chuckled. 'If I play dumb they'll just blame my programming. Anyway, you got Paul back and that's worth any amount of telling off.'

Ting! The lift stopped and Carrie drove out. Before long she put the brakes on, and the plates rattled overhead. 'Checkpoint ahead,' said Carrie.

'Thanks, we'll –'

'Uh-oh. Keep quiet a minute.'

Hal and Alex exchanged a glance. What was wrong? Then they heard it, getting louder and louder . . .

Thud, thud, thud!

Reece's footsteps! The robot had chased them all the way to A-section, and he was still after them!

THUD, THUD, THUD!

'Ponder my petabytes. Stop! Stop!'

Hal willed the trolley on, hoping she could outdistance the robot. Instead, she came to a stop.

'Yes? What is it?'

'It's Paul, isn't it?'

'No, I'm Carrie.'

'I don't believe you!' muttered Reece. Hal drew back as one corner of the tablecloth was lifted up. He realised Reece was looking for the buckled wheel, and he hoped the robot didn't crouch down for a really close inspection. If he did, he'd spot Hal and Alex right away.

'Do you mind?' snapped Carrie. 'I'll report you for that!'

'Pootle my power cord! My apologies madam, I thought you were someone else.'

'I should think so,' said Carrie, with a sniff.

Reece charged past at full speed, and Hal grabbed the edge of the tablecloth before it could flap up and reveal them sitting inside the trolley. Carrie set off after him, but barely two seconds later . . .

'Halt!' said a voice. It came from further up the passageway, and Hal realised it was Stinky's brother Richard.

'Make way!' shouted Reece. 'Thieves. Robbers! Emergency!'

'Stop where you are,' shouted the voice.

Thud, thud . . . thud.

The footsteps came to a halt as Reece obeyed the order to stop. Then Carrie arrived at the checkpoint, stopping right alongside the robot. Hal could actually see its gleaming feet through a gap in the tablecloth.

Beep beep! 'Delivery for the meeting room,' said Carrie brightly.

'Wait your turn,' said Richard importantly. 'I have to deal with the emergency first.'

'This . . . emergency,' said Carrie, using a halting computer voice. 'Quick, smart, fast. Rush delivery.'

'Doesn't look like it. Those plates are empty!'

'Urgent h-hurry,' stammered Carrie. 'Programming fault. Need to collect . . . other plates. Urgent. Overheat.'

Richard backed away. 'Go on, move. You're cleared!'

The motor whirred and Carrie was out of there

in seconds. As they drew away Hal heard Richard addressing Reece.

'Now tell me,' he said importantly. 'What's all this about thieves?'

There was a knot in Hal's stomach as the trolley rolled away from the checkpoint. They were heading deeper into A-section, site of the top secret labs! Stinky once joked that you needed special clearance just to mention the place, but his remark didn't seem so funny now. The space station was deadly serious about security, and zooming through the labs inside a runaway trolley wasn't exactly what Hal's parents meant by 'acceptable behaviour'. In fact, 'criminal behaviour' was more like it.

'Carrie, can you drop us off?'

'Not right now,' murmured the trolley. 'The security cameras are watching.'

Hal swallowed. Cameras! They didn't have those in the rest of the station, and the thought of hidden eyes recording his every move was disturbing. Even so, he was tempted to take a look. He only had to lift the tablecloth to see part of A-section. Stinky and the others would surely make him leader of the new gang after that!

Hal reached for the fabric, hesitated, then raised it the tiniest fraction. The view wasn't exactly encouraging - there was a corridor exactly like the ones in the rest of the Space Station, with grey-painted walls and unmarked doors. Then Carrie drove past a couple of technicians, and Hal gaped at the sight. They were dressed in bright orange hazard suits, and they were carrying big domed helmets under their arms. He caught a glimpse of their faces, and saw they were wearing identical pairs of dark glasses, with thick round lenses and little antennae on each side. The techs certainly didn't look like they were researching a new type of food, and Hal dropped the tablecloth in a hurry, glad they hadn't seen him. He was starting to wish they'd waited for Grogan at the checkpoint.

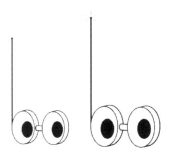

A few moments later Carrie got Hal's attention. 'Guard post ahead. Be silent.'

Another guard post! Would they search the food trolley? Hal and Alex exchanged worried glances.

Carrie stopped, and one of the guards cleared his throat. 'Now then, what's your game?'

'I don't understand,' said Carrie. 'What is a game?'

'Why are you carrying empty plates back into the meeting?'

'I'm just following orders,' said Carrie. She didn't mention they were Hal's orders.

The guards conferred in low voices. Following orders was something they were familiar with, but would they let the trolley through?

'All right, you can go in.'

The guards stood aside and the trolley started to roll again, gathering speed slowly as the motor struggled with the weight. They turned sharp right almost immediately, and Hal heard the familiar *whiiiish!* of automatic doors. They were entering the meeting room!

— 25 —

Ring Tone

Carrie came to a halt at the back of the meeting room, and the first thing Hal heard was Grogan's voice.

'Next, I'd like to thank you for this wonderful lunch. I know your resources are limited, but you did a pretty good job under the circumstances.'

There was a smattering of polite applause, but someone near the trolley whispered 'ungrateful swine'. There was muted laughter, and Hal glanced at Alex to see whether she'd heard.

'Now, to business. As you know, I'm visiting the Space Station to discuss your future. I believe there was some talk about a large donation which would help your research.'

The applause was louder this time.

'Unfortunately, you've been misinformed.'

There was a lot of murmuring from the audience.

'For the past two years this Space Station has been propped up with funds from twelve local planets. Their money has kept your research going, but that's about to stop.'

The audience gasped, and Hal heard his mum's voice close by. 'What are you talking about? We have funding for the next three years.'

'Not any more. They need the money for hospitals and schools.' VIP hesitated. 'That's the bad news. The good news is that the Space Station won't be closing down.'

There were sighs of relief.

'Why not?' asked Hal's mum.

'I've put together a short presentation. Lights please.'

In the darkness Hal was able to lift the tablecloth, and he and Alex peeped out. The audience were sitting at long tables covered with snowy white cloths, and silver cutlery gleamed under delicate candlelight. Hal spotted his mum, and he stared. Instead of the usual labcoat, she was wearing a blue evening dress, and her hair was arranged in plaits and tied up with a ribbon. As he looked around he recognised some of the other scientists and administrators, and they too were dressed to the nines. Hal's gaze returned to the candles and he frowned to himself. Oh, so it was okay for adults to light fires aboard the Space Station, was it? Typical!

Then he noticed the screen, just visible between the seated audience, and he settled down to watch. First there was a flashy logo and a burst of classical music, and then a wide-angle shot of the Space Station. The voiceover started as the camera got closer.

'Welcome to Space Hotel Oberon, the jewel in the Ezy-stae chain. With two hundred quality rooms, five restaurants and a zero-gravity plunge pool, your family will enjoy the vistas of space from the comfort of ten-star luxury.'

There was a commotion around the table, and Hal's mum leapt up. 'You can stop that nonsense right now,' she said, gesturing at the operator. The image vanished, and she turned to Grogan. 'I'm sorry you wasted your time coming here, and I hope you have a safe trip home. I'll have someone find your daughter and –'

'Now don't be hasty,' said Grogan. 'At least watch the rest.'

'There's no point.' Hal's mum glared at him, her eyes as hard as diamonds in the candlelight. 'Nobody is turning our home into a hotel!'

The other scientists nodded in agreement.

Grogan spread his hands. 'It's going to happen whether you like it or not. I'm here to explain how it'll work, and to find out which of you want to stay aboard after the handover.'

'Stay aboard?'

'Sure! We'll need managers, receptionists, tour guides, waiters ... the list is endless. You're all used to living in space so you'll get first pick of the jobs.'

Hal exchanged a glance with Alex, who looked as shocked as he did.

'Grogan, this is all nonsense,' said Hal's mum sharply. 'This research station is owned by the governments of twelve planets. You couldn't get them to agree on the time of day, let alone handing over control of the Space Station.'

'That's where you're wrong. It's taken three years and millions of credits, but I have a contract signed and verified by every planet.'

'I don't believe a word of it. Where are these documents?'

'My daughter has them.' Grogan accessed his wrist computer, and out the corner of his eye Hal saw Alex doing the same. He realised she was frantically hunting through the menus, looking for the mute button, but she was too late. A cheerful song rang out and her watch began to flash.

And everyone in the meeting room heard it.

For a split second Hal thought they might be able to get away. Carrie could move faster than any human, and once outside they could flee A-section at top speed. Even the guards outside could be dealt with, as long as Carrie played along.

But no. Before he could give the order, Alex stepped out of the trolley to face the music. There was no way Hal was letting her take all the blame, so he stood alongside, head held high.

There was an immediate uproar.

'Children . . . in A-section!'

'It's an outrage!'

'Shouldn't be allowed!'

'Never heard such a thing!'

161

'HAL JUNIOR. COME HERE THIS INSTANT!'

Hal barely recognised his mum's voice. He thought she was really angry when Grogan was threatening to take the Oberon away, but this was something else. She looked like she could bend steel bars with her bare hands, knock planets out of orbit at a glance AND eat three mouldy ration bars at a single sitting. And she was angry at *him!*

'Explain yourself at once!' thundered his mum. 'You know the rules. A-section is off limits!'

'It's my fault,' said a voice nearby.

Hal turned to see Alex holding the briefcase. 'My father needed this in a hurry, and I asked Hal to get me here as soon as possible.'

'Well yes . . . ' began Hal's mum. 'But the rules –'

Grogan cleared his throat. '*I* set the rules now, and my daughter can go anywhere she likes.'

'It's for their own safety!' said Hal's mum. 'Our research is very dangerous, and –'

'And it's been cancelled, as of today. I'll oversee the shutdown after lunch, but first let me show you the letter of agreement.'

Hal's stomach tightened, and he could almost feel the folded paper burning a hole in his pocket. Grogan had a nasty temper and his mum was already livid, and no matter what he did one of them was going to be even madder still.

— 26 —

Missing Sheet

Alex handed her dad the briefcase, and he made a big show of taking out a key and turning it in the lock. There was a loud click, and Grogan smiled as he took out the report. 'I'll leave this with you later. It might change your mind about staying on.'

'Fat chance,' snapped Hal's mum.

There was dead silence as Grogan flipped back and forth through the report. He did it again, more slowly, and then he frowned. 'Where is it? Who took it?'

'Where's what?'

'The letter of agreement!' Grogan scowled around the room. 'This is outrageous! One of you must have gone through my briefcase!'

'We've been with you the whole time,' said Hal's mum calmly. 'Perhaps you forgot to pack it?'

Grogan turned to his daughter. He looked furious.

'Alex, did you open my briefcase?'

'No,' said Alex firmly. 'Definitely not.'

'Did you let it out of your sight?'

Alex hesitated. 'I–'

'Tell me what happened! Who took it?'

'Nobody! Dad, I swear!'

Alex's face was very red, and Hal realised she was close to tears. He gripped the folded piece of paper in his pocket and looked away. If he gave up the contract Alex's dad would forgive her, eventually, but the Space Station would be lost. On the other hand, if he kept the piece of paper in his pocket the Space Station might be saved . . . but Alex would be in terrible trouble. It was an impossible decision!

Grogan threw the report into his briefcase and snapped it shut. His face was pale, his mouth a thin line, and he kept frowning at Alex as though he couldn't wait to get the whole story out of her. Nobody said a word, and the silence dragged on as Grogan gathered his things. Finally, he was ready.

'It took me six months to get those signatures,' he said in a tightly-controlled voice. 'That's wasted half a year of my busy life, but don't think I'll give up. I'll be back with another contract and you'll all be out.' Grogan glanced at Alex. 'As for you, you can forget about summer holidays. You're going to work in one of my factories, sunrise 'til sunset, until you learn some responsibility.'

Hal couldn't take it any more. 'Leave her alone! It wasn't her fault!'

Everyone stared at him, and he nearly backed down under the battery of intense looks. Quickly he pulled the folded contract from his pocket, opening it up with a rustle of thick paper. 'Here, I took your stupid papers. It was nothing to do with Alex!'

Grogan whisked the contract from his hand and held it up for Hal's mum to read. She tried to take it, but he moved it out of reach. Instead, she was forced to read the print from a distance, her jaw clenched. She looked angrier than ever, and Hal wondered whether she would challenge Grogan to a duel.

But Grogan was all smiles now. He'd won the battle, and he even put his arm around Alex and gave her a hug. 'I hope everything is in order?' he said, waving the contract. 'I won't ask you to move out straight away, but the workers will need quarters by the end of the month.'

Hal's mum was still trying to read the contract.

'Well?' demanded Grogan.

'You have a dozen signatures, and the wording is correct. Nice piece of paper too. Very smart.'

'Of course.' Grogan gave her a grin. 'A ten star hotel deserves the very best.'

'It's very impressive, but it's not worth the paper it's written on.'

'What ... what are you talking about?' Grogan stared at the contract. 'It's signed by the governments of all twelve planets!'

'I can see that. The problem is, you're short one signature.'

'Where ... which ... whose?'

'The thirteenth planet. Ours.' Hal's mum gave Grogan a beautiful smile, her eyes shining in the candlelight. 'Didn't anyone tell you? Space Station Oberon has its own constitution. We're a self-governed planet.'

'That's a lie!'

'No, it's perfectly true. Without our approval that paperwork is useless, and I guarantee the Station

Commander will never sign it. You might as well tear it up right now.'

Hal's spirits soared, and he couldn't wait for Grogan's reaction. Would he stamp his foot? Throw a tantrum? Vanish in a puff of yellow smoke?

Instead, Grogan took the contract in both hands, and for a split second it looked like he was going to shred it before their eyes. Then he laughed. 'Nice try with that thirteenth planet nonsense, but I know a desperate bluff when I hear one. This contract is perfectly valid.'

Hal stared at his mum, willing her to fight back, but when her shoulders dropped he realised it was all over. She'd given up! Grogan had won!

— 27 —

Candle Power

Ten minutes later the room was nearly empty. The scientists had left, heading to the labs to shut down their experiments, and the administrators had trooped out discussing severance pay and superannuation. Now only a handful of people remained: Hal's mum, Grogan, Alex and Hal, plus a couple of guards at the door.

'Take a seat, kids,' said Grogan heartily. 'Let me get you some ice cream!'

Hal felt sick to the stomach, and he shook his head. Alex didn't say a word.

'I said take a seat! I don't want you hovering around while I'm discussing business.'

Hal obeyed, sitting right between Grogan and his mum. If they started fighting he figured he might be able to stop them.

'Now, let's have some coffee.' Grogan snapped his

fingers and one of the guards looked in. 'Coffee, and make it instant.'

'As you wish,' said the guard.

Grogan smiled around the table. 'There, isn't that better?'

Three surly, angry and unhappy faces said otherwise. There were several candles on the table, but instead of softening the expressions they threw them into stark relief.

'So Hal, are you looking forward to Gyris? You'll be able to live in a proper house and play outside. Won't that be great?'

'I guess.' Hal stared into the nearest candle, lost in the flickering flame. He'd often dreamed of living on a real planet, but the Space Station was his home. If they turned it into an expensive hotel, he could never come back.

'And what about school? You'll have a real teacher, and –'

Hal's mum interrupted. 'You've won, Grogan. Stop teasing him.'

'I'm just grateful to the lad.' Grogan waved the letter of agreement, which gleamed in the candlelight. 'Without his help, this might have been lost for good.'

Hal scowled. He didn't need reminding.

'So, Hal. I hear you like camping?'

'Never tried it,' said Hal curtly.

'Come on Hal,' said his mum. 'Surely you remember practising for the trip to Gyris? You and Stin–, I mean, you and Stephen in the kitchen, trying to cook that ration bar? How we all laughed!'

... hmmm!

Laughed? Hal frowned. What was his mum on about? He'd been sent straight to his room after setting fire to . . . Oh! Hal's gaze travelled from the flickering candle to the letter of agreement and back again. 'Yes, mum. It tasted horrible after we cooked it. Worse than usual.'

'Plenty of fresh food on Gyris,' said Grogan heartily. 'You can have a barbecue every day!'

At that moment one of the guards came back with a steaming cup of coffee. Grogan reached forward to take it, the letter of agreement still clasped in his free hand, and as he did so Hal moved the candle underneath it. One corner of the paper curled and blackened, and there was a tiny wisp of smoke.

170

Unfortunately Grogan sat back in his chair before the paper caught, and his movement shifted the letter out of the flame. Grogan sniffed his coffee and made a face, but didn't notice the smouldering paper.

Hal muttered under his breath. He'd come so close but it hadn't worked.

Alex, who was seated opposite, had seen the whole thing. 'Dad, you forgot the sugar.'

'Eh? Oh yes.' Grogan reached forward, and the letter moved close to the candle again. Hal pushed it underneath and . . . success! The flames started to spread and he turned to his mum quickly.

'Mum, can I get a pet?'

'What?'

'When we're living on Gyris, can I get a pet dog?'

'I don't know, I –'

Hal never got the answer, because at that moment there was an angry roar behind him. Grogan pushed his chair back and leapt up, shaking the letter like mad to try and put it out. Unfortunately this made it burn even brighter, and the flames glowed blue and purple as they consumed the fancy paper.

'That'll be the enriched oxygen,' said Hal's mum. 'Fires burn a lot hotter aboard the Space Station, and they're awfully hard to put out. Isn't that right,

Hal?'

Grogan dropped his precious letter on the floor and stamped on it, but by the time he finally put the flames out only blackened fragments remained. He scooped up the pieces and tried to fit them back together, then turned on Hal. 'You did this! You set fire to my letter!'

'Utter nonsense,' said Hal's mum. 'He was talking to me.'

Grogan turned to Alex next, but she was sitting on the other side of the table and couldn't possibly have reached the candle. Furious, he crumbled the charred paper in his bare hands.

'Looks like your plans went up in smoke,' said Hal's mum. 'Now, would you like another coffee before you go home?'

❖

Before they left the meeting room Hal's mum beckoned to the guards. 'Shut down corridors Alpha through Epsilon, and warn everyone to close their doors. We're bringing these two through.'

'I could wear a blindfold,' said Hal.

'That won't be necessary.'

A few minutes later one of the guards came back. 'The area is secured.'

'Thanks, Jim. You two can take a break now.'

Hal kept his eyes peeled all the way to the checkpoint, hoping to find something interesting he could tell Stinky about. Unfortunately the corridor was totally bare, and he realised he'd have to make something up instead.

They arrived at the checkpoint, where Stinky's brother Richard was still on duty. He spotted Hal and Alex, and his eyes widened in surprise. 'You don't have passes for this section. How did you get through the checkpoint?'

'It was a real Carrie-on,' said Hal, and he heard Alex smother a laugh.

Two more corners and they lost sight of A-section. Hal was just telling himself the drama was over for the day when he heard a familiar sound.

Thud-thud-thud.

Hal and Alex exchanged a glance and hid behind the adults. They'd recognise those footsteps anywhere.

THUD-THUD-THUD!

Reece came charging round the corner, arms and legs pumping. 'Make way, make way. I'm chasing thieves!' Then he spotted Hal, and he let out a triumphant cry. 'Call the guards! I've found him,

I've found him!'

'What are you talking about?' demanded Hal's mum.

Before Reece could reply he spotted the briefcase in Grogan's hands. He snatched it in a flash, and a split second later there was only a fading *THUD-thud-thud* to prove he'd been there at all.

Grogan stared at his empty hand. 'Is this place completely out of control?' he asked, his voice dripping acid. 'That was a brand new briefcase!'

'Reece is our disposal expert. He collects rubbish and turns it into something useful.' Hal's mum looked Grogan up and down. 'You're lucky he only took the briefcase.'

◆

A few minutes later they arrived at the docking bay, and what a contrast! Earlier that day most of the the inhabitants of Space Station Oberon had turned out to welcome the important VIP and his 'son', Alex. And now, barely four hours later, Grogan's farewell audience consisted of one cleaner and a bored security guard.

'Don't walk on that bit,' protested the cleaner. 'I just mopped it!'

Grogan ignored him and strode through the middle. The cleaner shook his mop at Grogan's retreating back, and the security guard smiled to herself.

Meanwhile, Hal and his mum were saying their goodbyes to Alex.

'I know your dad is angry with us,' said Hal's mum. 'Just remember you're welcome here any time.'

Alex smiled gratefully.

'Will you be all right?' asked Hal. 'At home, I mean?'

'Sure. He gets annoyed when a deal falls through, but then he starts on the next one and everything's fine again.' Alex hesitated. 'Let me know when you're coming to Gyris, okay? I'll show you all the sights.'

Hal glanced at his mum. Was his punishment lifted, or was that visit to A-section going to cost him dearly?

'We'll talk about that later,' she said, her face stern.

Later. Hal's spirits sank. That meant no.

Alex saw his disappointment, and she took the watch off her wrist and held it out. 'Here. This is for you.'

Hal's eyes went round, but he shook his head. 'I can't take that. It's yours.'

'Go on. I insist.'

'But I don't have anything to give you!'

Alex smiled. 'You gave me an adventure. Who could ask for more?'

Slightly dazed, Hal took the watch, which was still warm from her wrist. Then it started flashing, and he almost dropped it.

'Uh-oh, that's my dad. I'd better be going.'

'Goodbye, then.' Hal put his hand out awkwardly, but Alex ignored it and leant in to give him a quick peck on the cheek.

'Until next time,' she whispered, and then she was gone.

Hal turned a bright flaming red, right up to the roots of his hair. Mortified, he glanced at his mum, but she was studying a speck of fluff on her lab coat. Hal breathed a sigh of relief. She hadn't seen a thing!

The new tutor

Hal woke early the next morning, fresh from a nightmare where Reece had been feeding him into the recycling machine. The robot had been pulling levers and cackling to himself, while his extra-large feet went *THUD THUD THUD* on the floor.

Hal shook himself. Hopefully the robot would leave him alone now it had the briefcase back.

Then he remembered . . . his mum had promised to think about the trip to Gyris overnight! Would it be yes or no?

Two minutes later Hal was running along the corridor, his hair a mess and his clothes half done up. He found his mum in the dining room, and she nodded at him as he ran in. 'Remind me to get you another comb,' she remarked, trying to smooth his hair.

'Mum . . . what about the camping trip?'

For a moment her face was stern, and then she smiled. 'It's all right, you can go. We could use the peace and quiet around here.'

'Yes!' Hal pumped his fist. The trip was on!

'There's just one thing. Your dad and I have decided to get you a tutor.'

Hal's face fell. More lessons? At this rate they'd wear his brain out before he got a chance to use it properly!

'We've found someone who will keep you in line. He's very capable, very strict, and he won't take any nonsense. Your grades should improve in no time, and your little exploits will be a thing of the past.'

Worse and worse, thought Hal gloomily. They might as well lock him up in prison! 'Mum, I can learn by myself!'

'I'm sure you can, but it's *what* you're learning that concerns me.' His mum glanced at her watch. 'Let's go to the canteen. There's someone I'd like you to meet.'

All of a sudden Hal put two and two together. A strict tutor who wouldn't take any nonsense . . . it couldn't be Reece, could it? Surely not!

They took the lift to the next level, and when the doors opened Hal hesitated before stepping out.

'Don't worry about Reece,' said his mum. 'We

shipped him back to Gyris. They're going to reprogram him as a parking inspector.'

Hal breathed a sigh of relief. Having Reece as a tutor would have been a living nightmare.

'Come on. I want to show you something.'

They turned the corner, and Hal almost fell over when he saw the entire population of the Space Station waiting in the canteen. The tables were laden with every delight Hal could imagine . . . and he could imagine quite a lot. There was a huge ham, glistening under the coloured lights, sliced meats and olives, crusty bread, bowls of salad and fruit, and a huge cake with his name on top. Unable to speak, Hal approached the tables, his eyes round. The crowd gave him three rousing cheers, and he had to turn away because a speck of dirt got into his eye.

The rest of the afternoon was a blur of friendly faces, slaps on the back, hearty handshakes and thank-yous. Everyone was happy and cheerful, including the *two* motorised trolleys who darted through the crowd serving drinks and sweets galore. Carrie gave him a happy beep as she sped past, and Paul showed off his brand new wheel.

Before long Hal had eaten so much food he felt like one of Teacher's math problems: if two grown ups can eat five cakes in three days, how many

179

cakes can one boy eat in an afternoon? About as many as Hal, that was the answer! And then, when he was full to bursting point, he sat back to enjoy the atmosphere.

As he was sitting there he heard footsteps approaching, and he saw a flash of bronze as a tall robot sat next to him. For a second he thought it was Reece, come to get him, but he realised it was a different model altogether. This robot was old and battered, but it had a friendly expression and warm yellow eyes.

'Hello. What's your job?' asked Hal.

'I used to be a pilot,' said the robot, in an even male voice. 'Now I'm a minder.'

'What does that mean?'

'I was hired to look after a particularly troublesome character,' said the robot, with a twinkle in his eye. 'A bit of a tearaway, by all accounts.'

Hal's mother spotted them together. 'I see you've met your new tutor.'

'Tutor!' Hal gaped at the robot. 'You're here for me?'

'Are you Hal Junior?'

'Y-yeah.'

'It's a pleasure to meet you,' said the robot, extending his hand.

They shook. 'Nice to meet you too, er ...' Hal eyed the faded black lettering on the robot's chest. 'XG99?'

'Oh, that's just my model name.' The robot smiled, crinkling the plasteel skin around his eyes. 'My friends call me Clunk.'

It was late at night and Hal was lying in bed, gazing through the porthole at the distant stars. His eyelids were drooping and he was struggling to stay awake, but he knew planet Gyris would be moving into view any minute. The planet would only be a bright little speck at this distance, but he still wanted to see it. His dad was there, organising the camping trip, and Alex would be home too. He wondered whether she would bother to look up. Could you see the Space Station from Gyris, or would it just be an insignificant dot in the rich starfield? Could you flash messages back and forth if you had a really bright light?

Moments later a blueish dot came into view at the far right of the porthole, and Hal knelt on the end of his bed to get a better look. His breath misted up the porthole, turning the stars into spiky diamonds, and he wiped it with his pyjama sleeve. There it was again, the rich blue planet he'd be visiting two days from now. Down there they had forests, rivers, mountains and cities with millions of people. They ate rich foods every day, and they could run and play outside. Swimming too, in real water.

The Space Station continued to turn, and the planet moved slowly across Hal's field of view. At that moment he realised it would be fantastic to visit Gyris and experience new adventures, but he could never live there. He belonged in space, and when he was grown up he'd pilot his own ship, just like Captain Spacejock of the Intergalactic Peace Force. Then he'd be able to visit planets at will, stopping wherever he pleased. That was the way to live!

Gyris was on the far left of the porthole now. Hal watched it disappear, then smiled to himself. Two days from now he wouldn't be staring at a tiny dot in space . . . he'd be landing on it. And wouldn't the camping trip be something to remember?

He laid down and pulled the blanket up to his chin, and just before he fell asleep he remembered his new tutor. Clunk said he used to be a pilot, and Hal wondered whether he could talk the robot into a few flying lessons.

Now that would really be something!

Acknowledgements

To Pauline Nolet, to Ian and to Jo and Tricia
thanks for the awesome help and support!

Thanks also to the keen readers
at Rosalie Primary School.

The Hal Junior series ...

The *first* book in the Hal Junior series!

Don't forget ...

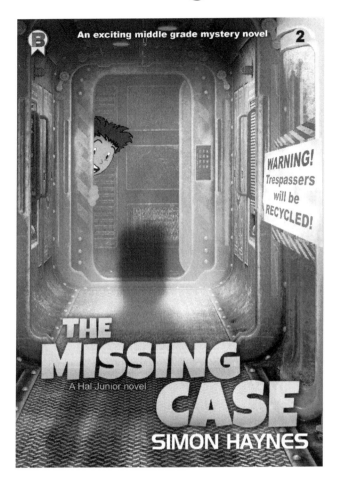

An exciting middle grade mystery novel

2

WARNING!
Trespassers
will be
RECYCLED!

THE
MISSING
A Hal Junior novel
CASE

SIMON HAYNES

The *second* book in the Hal Junior series!

And ...

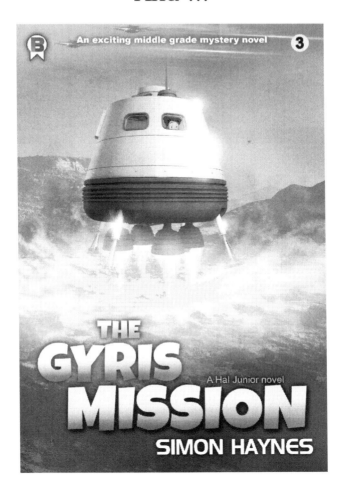

An exciting middle grade mystery novel 3

THE
GYRIS
MISSION

A Hal Junior novel

SIMON HAYNES

The *third* book in the Hal Junior series!

And ...

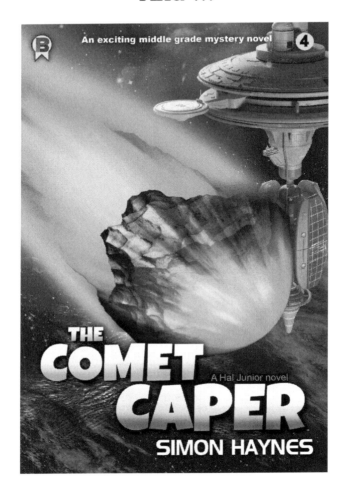

The *fourth* book in the Hal Junior series!

If you enjoyed this book, please leave a brief review at your online bookseller of choice. Thanks!

About the Author

Simon Haynes was born in England and grew up in Spain. His family moved to Australia when he was 16.

In addition to novels, Simon writes computer software. In fact, he writes computer software to help him write novels faster, which leaves him more time to improve his writing software. And write novels faster. (www.spacejock.com/yWriter.html)

Simon's goal is to write fifteen novels before someone takes his keyboard away.

Update 2018: goal achieved and I still have my keyboard!

New goal: write thirty novels.

Simon's website is spacejock.com.au

Printed in Great Britain
by Amazon